DIVERGENCE

Todd Misura

BEG

CHAPTER 1

I was looking forward to the weekend, just me and some games for tonight and Saturday and then maybe I'd go out on Saturday night or Sunday morning. I had already cashed my check and was headed home. I worked construction at this time of my life. It was back breaking labor, in the hot sun of Arizona all day. I loved the country side, but only felt good here during the winters where it was normally in the fifties or sixties at the most. I was sweating as I pulled my beat to hell car into the apartment parking lot, looking forward to resting. I checked the mail and threw the unimportant stuff in the trash can next to the boxes on the bottom floor. I took the stairs because the elevator was slower and I took my time. I wasn't out of shape; it was just hot the higher you went up because of the lack of shade on the building. Today had reached around 101 and I knew that my apartment was waiting for me, a quiet and cold cave all for me.

When I first saw her she dropped her purse and was scrambling to find her glasses. I was two doors down on the right side of the hall, so I walked over and picked them up. I handed them to her and she slipped them on. Her hair was a mess and her face was pouring sweat. I was too and I was itching to get into my apartment. Living on the fourth of five floors was hot, but I had air conditioners in every room with big enough windows. The four machines made it like an ice box and I loved it. Some nights when it got cool enough outside, my windows would fog and I'd see my breath.

I turned and walked back to my small place and she called out.

"Thank you! Most people don't notice me!"

I turned back to her and smiled, our eyes locked. Her glasses were thick, and they magnified her eyes several times. It was strange looking at them, but I kept my gaze on her for a few seconds as I turned back to my place. I looked her over. Her small breasts stood out against her stomach, which bulged slightly as if she was three or four months pregnant. I didn't think she was, because she wasn't straining as hard as I would think a pregnant woman would in this heat. She was attractive in a subtle way, not my usual type. She was tall, about six feet almost, and her long hair was curly, the bones in her hands and wrists stood out. She was skinnier than I ever liked. I've always preferred girls with a heft to them. Something about her made me curious, she felt… different.

I've experienced what are called supernatural or cryptic creatures before, the worst being an energy vampire I ran into one night when I was drunk. He found me stumbling down a back alley, trying to get to my apartment, and he offered to help.

"Friend, you look like you need a hand. Take my arm." He offered his almost hairless arm for me to wrap around, and I did. I was getting over a bad breakup and I thought drinking would help. It hadn't and it kicked my ass. I let this strange man guide me to my street, and the ten to fifteen minutes he walked me he asked questions.

"Was she beautiful to you?"

"God yeth. See was so hot in beed. I have 'er all I 'ad."

"Did she hurt you?"

"Bith left me for a – a woman!"

"Oh, that must have hurt worse than her leaving you for a bigger cock, eh?"

"Thas I understand. I'm okith sized. 'Bout seven by three. 'Unny angled."

Then it got strange. I remember walking us up to the door of the complex. I remember thinking he looked really hot. He was tall, built under the leather duster he wore in the heat. His peroxide white hair stood out against the black of the leather. He wasn't sweating, and he wanted to come in.

"Thanx for 'elping me. Good damn I'm drunk. Wanna come in?"

The freak stood there, nodding silently. I remember making it up halfway and when I woke up the next morning I knew I had been used by him. It wasn't sexually, except for the blow job he offered. I felt used up in my soul, like a void had been swapped out instead of having my heart and soul in my core. I sat there, feeling like I was falling into a black hole for the next day or two, sleeping fitfully, crying constantly. I didn't know what to do, a black wall of despair was rising in me, darker than I'd ever felt before. By the next night around ten o'clock I knew something was wrong with me. Then it hit me, the conversation, the beej, it was an energy vampire feeding off me.

I had got up suddenly, now driven to fix my situation. I lit a smoke and as I held the tobacco in my lungs, I rushed around gathering materials. I grabbed the sea salt, crushed red peppers, pure white candles and fresh matches. The candles were small votives that had their own glass holders. I set two in front of the door and two at every window. Sprinkling a mixture of the salt and peppers around the candles I lit them. I prayed to the Lord and Lady, asking for protection from the vampire.

After the candles were lit and my prayers sent to the universe, I drew a hot bath. Dumping the rest of the sea salt into the hot water, I climbed in. I scooped up some salt and started scrubbing my skin, from head to toes. I felt the despair grow more and more as I placed the protection spell and candles around the apartment. A large part of me knew I should just kill myself; Jenny had done this to me. Jenny had destroyed my life, why live?

I knew then, as I slipped into the water and scooped up the

salt that I had been marked. I felt the link breaking as I scrubbed down and when I was done, I climbed out. Dressing in fresh clothes, I knew I was safe, the link was broken.

Blinking the memory away now, I opened my door. The cold air met me at the door frame, and a little bit of condensation billowed out at the bottom of the door frame. I smiled to myself about helping her and then I went about my night.

While I was in the middle of a difficult boss battle I heard the doorbell ring. I got up, pausing the game, actually a little grateful for the interruption. I lit a smoke as I answered the door and when I opened it, I saw it was her. She was holding a small casserole dish that had a mix of stuff in it. It looked like macaroni, green olives, cheese and hamburger. I stepped out of the way of the door and motioned her in.

"I know this is strange, but I made you dinner. I hope you don't mind…" The dish was wrapped in potholders, and it looked hot.

"No! I mean-I don't mind. I was getting ready to make something for myself; I guess you beat me to it. I needed a break anyways."

I motioned her to set it on the counter. I got two bowls and a serving spoon out, set them next to the potholders and dish that rested on them. I handed her a bowl. In the chilly air there was steam rising off of it. It seemed to swirl around her face, clinging to her.

She took it and stood there, shivering.

"Are you cold? I can turn off one of the air conditioners if you like." I walked over to the small one in the kitchenette. She nodded, still shivering. Her hands were wrapped around the bowl but I noticed that she seemed to do it less after I turned it off. I pointed at the barstool at the counter top and I hopped on the other one. We ate slowly; the food must have just come from the oven. It was interesting and I never thought that it would be. The green olives and cheese mingled, the tartness of the olives complimenting the saltiness of the cheese. I wanted to learn how to make it.

"Wow. This is really good! I've not had a good home cooked meal in ages. I'm so sorry, I'm Jerry. Sorry I didn't mention that earlier."

"Irvina, nice to meet you Jerry." She seemed to stand up a bit taller after my honest complement of her cooking. It was really good, and I wanted more. I couldn't eat it fast enough because of how hot it was, but it was fresh food. I planned on some crappy rice bowl or two, not a filling meal by any stretch.

We stood there in silence, it was a bit strange. I looked over at her, she was wearing a solid blue t-shirt and the same pants from earlier. Her skin glowed blue in the dark apartment, the screen lighting her skin up. I could see her curly red hair was still down, and I wanted to run my hands through it. I jumped a little at that though, and I kept stealing glances at her. She didn't seem as thin as I originally thought. She was also cuter than I originally thought. She had a Western European look to her, from strange places like Prague or Russia. Her eyes were a dark purple color, almost unnatural, and they were focused on her bowl of food. Her glasses were different, but it didn't seem to deter my mind from thinking I'd been a dick earlier when I wrote her off.

She was still shivering slightly and I felt bad. I pulled the blanket off the back of the couch and handed it to her. I held her bowl as she wrapped it around her, and I handed it back.

I ate more of my food, it cooled in the chilly air, and I got more in my bowl. I was staring at the paused screen. It was a boss I'd been fighting for awhile that I couldn't seem to get past. She looked over at it as if she didn't know what it was.

"I was in the middle of a boss battle, and I needed a break. It's a video game."

"What's a video game?" Her thin, arched eyebrows raised

in interest and confusion.

"Seriously? You don't know what they are? Come on, I'll show you!"

Lighting a smoke as I entered the living room, I pointed to the couch. I picked up the controller and started trying the boss again. I got my ass beat in several hits and it restarted. I paused as the level started again. Irvina was sitting next to me, about two or three feet away and she was lost in the colors and violence on the screen. I could tell that she was having a difficult time deciphering what she was seeing. I didn't know where she came from, or her history. I started to wonder if she was an escapee from a religious cult or something.

Taking a few minutes to explain how the controller worked and how you played the game, I resumed and started whacking at the boss. The first several forms of it were simple, but I was frustrated quickly. Dying once again, I took it to the main screen of the system, fired up a 16-bit classic, *Sonic*, and handed the controller to her. She looked at it, her magnified eyes wide in wonder, and she fumbled her way to the first level. I got up, letting her explore the game and entered the kitchen. Stubbing out my third smoke in the ashtray on the counter I put the extra food in a clean bowl and into the fridge.

"Oh! The rings let me get hit!" She giggled in surprise at figuring it out herself, and she tapped a few buttons before she paused it. She turned and smiled at me, and I had to smile back.

"Yep! Collect a hundred of them and you get an extra life. I'll be in there in a few." I washed up the bowls and her casserole dish, dried them off, and carried her potholders and dishes into the living room. Going back into the kitchen I grabbed a cup of coffee and sat on the couch next to her. She had been squealing in delight while I had my back to her and she was already on the third level, she really had it figured out. I sat there, drinking my coffee and watching her play.

She ran out of lives and it went to the continue screen. She handed the controller over to me, and I flipped the machine off. She turned towards me, and quickly kissed me on the cheek. I had a few days growth, and I hoped it didn't scratch or irritate her. She stood, grabbed her things and turned towards me, leaning over a little. Her shirt dropped and I saw her breasts swinging free under it. I snapped my eyes to hers and she smiled.

"Thank you! I had a wonderful time!"

"Good, Irvina, I want you to know if I'm home you can come over, ok?"

Her eyes got impossibly big at that statement, and to my surprise, her eyes watered up. She stood for a moment and bolted for the door. I jumped up, unsure of what I said to make her cry. She flung the door open and slammed it as she left. The sound pissed me off irrationally, and I forced it out because I didn't want to ruin this odd, but exciting thing fleeting through me.

I flopped back down on the couch, unsure of what I wanted to do. I kept thinking of her breasts swinging free under her shirt, how I didn't see her nipples get hard the whole time she was here despite the cold. I shook my head, thinking that I must have fucked up somehow. I stood after smoking a few more cigarettes and headed for the shower.

I grabbed some clothes from the bedroom and entered the bathroom where I slipped my clothes off, throwing them into the washer before I pulled a towel from the dryer. Climbing in the shower, I blasted myself with hot water. I hated sweating, I was a construction worker and it's all I did when I was there. I started with my hair, scrubbing and rinsing quickly. I started lathering up my arms, squeezing and massaging the muscles in my biceps. I wasn't vain, but the muscles I had from my job impressed me. I always had muscular calves, but lifting several hundred pounds of material every half hour or so toned them even more.

Irvina kept coming to mind. I had gotten a good look at her

while we ate. She wasn't pregnant as far as I could tell. Her hair was a deep red that I thought was dyed. Her eyes were a vibrant purple and I decided that was part of what made her hard to look at. They seemed to tractor beam your soul to hers. Her breasts seemed small, but the shirt she wore was a bit loose, so I couldn't tell. I was more curious about her than her body, I decided. The fact that she hadn't played video games freaked me out a little. Everyone who grew up in the last forty years knew what they were, right? Even with the strangeness of her, she turned me on. Maybe that was why she aroused me and my interest in her, her strangeness, and those eyes. They seemed to command the room and plead with it at the same time. There was power and a weakness in them.

While I was washing my groin, I got hard.

In my mind's eye I saw her going down on me in the shower, head bobbing forward and back as she sucked me off. I started jerking it, quick and efficiently, getting it done with. I felt strange, almost ashamed. I rinsed off and hopped out of the shower, I toweled off, dressed quickly, and threw open the bathroom door. The chill air rushed over me and I got goose bumps. I shivered enjoying the sensation. Monday was a holiday and this was Friday, so I had three days ahead of me.

I went to the fridge and got a drink, a hard iced tea. Walking back into my bedroom, I clicked on the computer and as it booted up, I lit a smoke. Sitting in my fancy office chair, I leaned back with my drink on the desktop. I rubbed my eyes, thinking of Irvina sucking me off in the shower. I didn't want to think about this, I'd just had…

I pushed that thought deeper into the back of my mind.

I fired up my browser and started checking my sites. I read through a few articles and posts, but I kept going back to Irvina. I wanted her, wanted her on her hands and knees on my bed. I wanted be pounding her hard and fast, hands on her hips, then her breasts. Gripping her shoulders tight as I fucked her harder.

Once again I was hard. I pushed away from the desk, going over to the bed; I flopped down on my back, staring at the ceiling. The smooth paint swirled around, my eyes playing tricks on me. I closed them and felt like I was on a merry go round.

I didn't know her; I didn't even notice her until today. I'd lived here for six years and I never knew that there was someone living in...415? I sat on the edge of the bed smoking for a few minutes before I registered what exactly I was doing. I was confused and a little shocked that I burned through several smokes without me realizing it. Frowning, I looked at the bedside clock. It was around 1am, and when she left and I got my shower it had only been around ten. Where the hell had time gone?

I stood, stretching and hearing my knees pop, I knew that I had been sitting there for a few hours. I walked over to the desktop and shook the mouse to wake it up. I downed the drink, warm and gross after sitting out for a few hours. Clicking off the computer, I went back into the living room, opened the fridge and grabbed two more before I headed for the couch. I set the drinks down on the coffee table before opening one and I pulled the drawer open to get out the novel that I'd been reading.

Reading and sipping, I read a couple of hours before I got tired enough to crawl off to bed. It was close to three am. Laying there in bed, with my eyes drifting closed I fell into a deep sleep.

CHAPTER 2

In my sleep, I dreamed of her. She was beautiful without the glasses, her eyes a purple that bore into my soul. There were only a few sexual dreams, but they were vivid and realistic. I kept seeing her slightly long torso against the bed, face buried in a pillow. She was screaming my name over and over. I wasn't sure if she was saying it out of pleasure or pain, but I was in her as deep as I could be. My hips were like pistons, thrusting hard enough to make her scoot forward every other thrust. Eventually her head was slapping against the wall, but I kept thrusting. Suddenly, she thrust back, and I was thrown off the bed, onto the floor. She was on top of me, her irises and hair pitch black.

"You're mine! I claim you! You are mine!"

She was screaming incoherently at me and her teeth were long fangs. Her black irises burned a hole in my soul, and her hands were talons digging into my chest. I screamed and I threw her off of me. I stood in front of the large mirror attached to my dresser.

I had scratches, long thin rivulets of blood. The burning sensation hurt and I realized I was awake. My sheet and comforter were on the floor and I was drenched in sweat. Irvina was nowhere to be found in the room and I was shaking. I prowled the apartment, looking everywhere. I was freaked out; sometimes I woke up to strange things: a loud boom in my left ear, weird things on my body or my front door open. It's been happening all of my life, and I always thought it was me sleep walking or just being a teen. I was checked out several times throughout my teens and early adulthood, but nothing had been explained. So, I dealt with it, keeping a log of all the events when I would remember them.

As a kid I'd wake up in the middle of the night with this feeling of being hurt or violated in some way. Finding bruises or scratches on me, my parents would ask me what the hell I was doing in my sleep. I always had an impression that something was going on, but I could never figure out what. The bruises were small and usually on my fingers, nose, or legs. Sometimes my feet would be dirty like I walked in the woods in my sleep, but growing up my mom never mentioned me missing from my room. I don't know what it meant, but alien abduction stories played out like this a lot. Things like this were not the best fears to have riled up in the middle of the night, not when there were claw marks on my chest. I was close to panicking, I looked at my fingers. They didn't have signs of being the culprit and I was concerned. Then it hit me.

The apartment was warm. I checked the air conditioners. They had been turned off, and it would take several hours before they would start to cool the apartment again. I fired them up to the highest settings and stalked back to my bed room where it was cooler. I had a thin sheen of sweat on my forehead and it irritated me more than the burning cuts on my chest. In front of my dresser mirror again, I checked my hands, but I didn't have fingernails that could scratch. I had a horrible habit of biting my nails, so it wasn't me. I lay on the bed, the standing fan blowing the cold air across my chest. The burning was going away and I was tired. It was about five in the morning and I wanted to get up around ten. I got comfortable and fell asleep, dreaming nothing.

I woke up at ten. I hopped in the shower and when the hot water hit the scratches they burned again. I washed them up really good, all six of them. I had three starting at my left pectoral and the same on the right side. The scratches just missed my nipples, as if the thing that scratched me didn't want to harm me there. I climbed out of the shower, careful of my chest. I didn't know what the hell happened to me. My mind kept wandering to

Irvina as I smoked my cigarette, and I made a decision.

I had to go talk to Irvina, but not about the strange night I had. I wanted to see if she wanted to come over, and hang out. I called a pizza place and ordered two large pizzas and wings, then I called down to the convenience store for a carton of smokes and case of hard iced tea. I paid over the phone with my credit card and they said they'd have it delivered in an hour. I fired up my coffee pot and lit my third smoke.

I sat at the counter, going over the strong sexual dreams that I had the night before. Thinking about it, I wanted her. I wanted to get to know her too, but the freaky shit at the end kept making me freeze, kept making me go what the hell was I thinking, maybe it was a sign. My chest hurt like hell off and on, but I decided to go over and ask. I got up, stubbing out my smoke, just as someone knocked.

It was Irvina, dressed in a loose t-shirt and a pair of jeans. Her eyes were red behind her coke bottle glasses and she looked like she hadn't slept.

"Can I come in?"

"Sure, sure."

I motioned her in and offered her a cup of coffee. She took it, shivering once she was in my apartment again. She wrapped her fingers around the mug, sucking the heat into her normal fingers. She sipped a few times and then took a large swig. The coffee put a color to her cheeks and I realized that she was pale. Her skin color was similar to someone who hadn't seen the sun for months. It made me wonder what exactly she had done before now, where she came from. The strange cult idea came back, but I was curious for the real answer.

"You're not from here are you? I think you're new to America, right?"

"Yes."

"You about my age? I'm thirty three. And you've not seen much of the world have you?"

She sat there, nodding in silence. I was scared that I would chase her off, but I said *fuck it* and asked.

"What happened? Why did you flee?"

"I'm not accustomed to people. This is the first time in my life that I've lived on my own. My parents and I lived in a house together until a year ago. When I first moved into the city I couldn't even shop for myself. I had a friend who would take me out to shop and eat. They've left me, but I can buy my own groceries and pay my bills without crying now!"

"Wow. What-" I whipped my head towards her, alarm rising on my face and in my chest.

"They're dead." She stiffened slightly then released a deep breath and relaxed.

I raised an eyebrow, but didn't press her for more info. I lit a smoke and offered her one. Surprisingly, she took one and lit it with her own lighter. She went cross-eyed while she watched the flame ignite her smoke, and I chuckled.

Her eyes snapped to mine, and her brow furrowed.

"What? Why are you laughing?"

"Want the truth? You looked cute with your eyes all funny as you lit that."

"Oh. I..."

I smiled at her and I drained my coffee cup. Motioning to the living room we moved to the couch. She sat next to me, about a foot between us. I fired up my console and she smiled. I started playing an online shooter, getting shot at left and right because I kept looking at her from the corner of my eye. She noticed and hid her smile behind her coffee mug. It was a Care Bears cup that my mom had, I'd kept it after she passed. Irvina's dark red hair was down, curling to her waist. It had been up last night, and I hadn't thought about it much other than if it was dyed. I wanted to say something, so I told her about my mom.

"I lost my mom when I was twenty. She passed away while making lunch one day. I stopped by an hour or so after she died and found her there."

"Death is a vicious bitch. She takes and takes and takes. She never gives. That's what the Goddess is for."

I sat there, surprised that she was pagan. I felt the necklace under my shirt. It had a bear claw set made of pewter and a pentacle in the center. I was pagan, but kept it to myself. I only knew what she was referring to vaguely because almost every pagan is different from another. We all have a common belief in a god or gods that meant something to us.

I didn't want to talk religion, I wanted to blow shit up and impress her.

She watched, bored after a few more minutes of me dying repeatedly. She made me smile though, realizing that I was starting to stare longer at her and that made her giggle. I was frustrated with the game and got up, letting my avatar die while I refilled her mug and mine. I came back and lit a smoke.

"Upper left, on the roof!"

She started calling out places where enemies were and it got me back to focus on the game. After the match was over, I turned towards her a little, I set the controller on the coffee table and my hands were on my knees.

"What do you want to do?"

"I don't know. This is kinda fun now."

I played another match, coming up to fifth place with Irvina's help. She called out positions from her perspective, while I was nailing shots and diving behind cover when she got scared I was going to die. I was laughing as the players were getting frustrated at me for suddenly jumping from fifth to second. The match ended, and all the previous players who were doing well left. I turned off the game and pulled up my Netflix.

"Movie?"

"No. I must be going for now. You want me to come back later?"

The door bell chimed and I hopped up. I had forgotten about the pizza and the supplies. I rushed to the door, and after checking the peephole, I realized that it was both deliveries. I pulled out my wallet and grabbed thirty dollars of loose money. I flung the door open and took the case of drinks, setting it on the floor. The carton was on top of the pizzas and I handed both of them 15 dollars each. They bade me a nice day, and I closed the door.

"I got two huge pizzas! Want some?"

Irvina moved behind me and she shook her head.

"No. I'll be back around five or so, maybe then?"

I frowned. I hoped she'd stay for at least a slice or two, but she was intent on leaving. I opened the door for her and as she gripped the outside handle I looked again at her fingers. They were normal, long and slender, the nails were trimmed neatly, and not the talons from the dream. Her eyes bore into me, but they were her hypnotic purple, nothing else. I glanced away, ashamed of the dreams that I'd had. As she was leaving and closing the door behind her, the claw marks on my chest hurt. It was a fire all of a sudden, and I winced. The door clicked closed silently, the air conditioners masking the quiet sound.

CHAPTER 3

I spent the rest of the day munching on pizza and drinking myself into a slight stupor playing games. It was close to about eight when I realized that either I missed Irvina or she'd not come back over. I was getting sleepy. I turned off the TV and the console, draining the current bottle. I had about eight, and the case was a thirty pack. I wasn't worried about running out, but I needed that nap. I crawled into bed and passed out.

I woke up and I glanced at my phone. It said three eighteen am, and I groaned. I was wide awake, and it was almost three thirty. I didn't have anything pressing, but I got up and ran to the bathroom. I pissed for an eternity and stumbled into the living room where I lit a smoke and glanced at the door. There was a small white envelope just past it, on the right side where the door and the latch met. I walked over to it, surprised how it had been slipped in. I picked it up, it smelled faintly of Irvina. Her apartment must have been scented too, because something that smelled of incense wafted from the interior of the envelope. It was a sharp smell, like cinnamon and musky spices, I liked it. The note was folded over twice.

It was simple and to the point.

I'll be awake till about 4-5 am. Please, stop by if you're awake then.

IRVINA

I looked at the note, unsure if I should set off to her place or not. Glancing down at my rumpled clothes, I shrugged to myself and decided I'd head over. I put out my smoke, grabbed my pack from the coffee table and grabbed my keys. I stepped into the warm hallway locking my door and then I noticed something strange.

On the far end of the hallway to my left there was a window and on the window were hundreds if not thousands of mosquitoes. Grossed out I headed over to her door and I knocked rather softly. I could smell the scents that infused the note and envelope through the door and I smiled. Her door popped open; she was standing there in a robe. My eyes locked on hers, she wasn't wearing her glasses. Her robe was only half closed, I had to struggle not to look at her left breast poking through, and then exposed as her robe slipped open more.

She smiled, and dragged me into her apartment.

CHAPTER 4

Her living room was lit entirely by votives and pillar candles. In the center of the room were several large pillows. She dragged me to the mound and pushed me to the floor. Her robe was off and her hands were on my belt before I even realized what was going on. My cock was hot in my boxers, pressed against my thigh. I felt the pre-come draining out of me. I wanted her bad, but holy fuck this was fast. My cock bobbed free from my pants and boxers and her mouth took me in.

For a moment I freaked, terrified of my dreams, but the sensations pulsing through my cock and balls made me ignore the dreams. I sat up a little and whipped my shirt off, throwing it near the door. She was bobbing fast and tight on me, tongue flicking across the underside of my cock, my hands deep in her hair. She was staring at me, our eyes locked as she bobbed and I started moaning loudly. She pulled away from me, eyes glittering in the candle light, the supernatural purple lit by fire. She was holding her breasts, cupping them and letting them bounce. I gasped in lust, and she put her hands on my thighs as she took me in her mouth again. My hands went to her hair, soft and silky, trying not to thrust up into her mouth.

I came, large amounts of semen coming from a seemingly hidden reservoir. I lost count after the second spurt, afraid that she would gag or choke on the amount. She swallowed it all, licking my tip as she pulled her mouth free. I lay there panting, gripping the pillows under me. The apartment was hot, hotter than normal. I was sweating profusely when I noticed the heat, but I didn't care. She slid atop me, moving past my groin so her ass was resting on my chest. Her unshaven groin was inches from my face and I could smell her. She smelled as exotic as her looks made her, and I wanted her. She sat there for several moments, my heartbeat pounding harder with each passing second. I didn't know what she wanted, or wanted me to do. I couldn't reach up and touch her because my arms were pinned under her legs. So I lay still. She started masturbating, her long middle finger and pointer rubbing her to a quick climax. Her fluids ran down my chest, and her smell grew stronger making me want her more.

"I want you."

"Not now. Tonight is my night. I choose what you get."

She raised herself from me then, and with two quick strides backwards her ass was over my cock, its tip brushing her ass cheeks. I resisted the urge to move, to thrust. She leaned down, her breasts pressing against my chest, ass away from my cock. We were staring into each other's eyes and I had no clue what was happening.

Her kisses were soft and fast, one after another on my lips, cheeks, shoulder. Then she and I met, lips pressing and I felt my breath slide from me. I exhaled as we kissed and she seemed to inhale it. I wanted more, and we kept passionately kissing. Lips pressing together wet and firm. I kept my arms to my sides, not wanting to spook or upset her. Her hands were around my head, on either side. I glanced quickly at her fingers, remembering the claws from my dream but they were normal.

Suddenly she sat up, our lips untwined.

Her hands on her hips, she stands, no balancing act required. Just a straight stand, and she stalked over to a closed doorway and looked back at me.

"Leave. Please."

I lay there blinking a few times, unsure if I heard her right.

"Please, leave me."

Realizing that she was serious, I scrambled to put myself

back in my shorts and grab my shirt. I was confused and a little upset. I wanted to know what I had done, but I was afraid to talk. I didn't know why, but I felt like talking would ruin everything that we accomplished together. Actually in that moment I felt ashamed of the sex, like I had done something wrong. I was sweating like crazy and when I stepped into the hall, pulling the door closed behind me, it was cool. The hallway was normally still warm in the middle of the night. I glanced at the mosquito covered window, but they were gone. So was the window, it had been shattered inwards. I didn't want to fuck with it, fuck with anything.

I pulled my key out and unlocked my door. The wave of cold mixed with the sweat made me shiver. I stepped in, and closed the door, locking it. I picked up the note from Irvina, but I couldn't discern anything off with the note or the tone.

I called and left a voicemail for the supervisor about the window, got two bottles of hard iced tea and some pizza slices from the fridge. I sat on my couch in the dark and ate. I fell asleep after my smoke, shivering.

It was dark and then a light appeared ahead of me. I moved towards it in my dream state, lucidly moving forward. The light was orange, and Irvina was in the center of it. She was on her knees, nude. She had her hands on her thighs and her eyes were closed. Her breathing was shallow, an even and meditative pace. I swirled around her and her eyes snapped open. They were black. Not just the iris, but the whole damn thing. She stared and launched herself at me. She passed through my ethereal form and spun around. She was trying to figure out what was going on and I saw something click in the shiny black of her eyes.

I snapped awake and my door shattered inwards. I leapt off the couch, dodging parts of the door flying towards me. She was standing there, nude. I felt my breath catch in my chest, her surreal beauty catching me off guard. Her eyes were not visible in the backlighting from the hallway, the light wrapped around her in a strange way. She was standing before me suddenly, and behind her the apartment was warping. It was fuzzy, like an out of focus film projector. Her eyes were pitch black and glossy and her hands wrapped around my throat. I couldn't breathe, and she started talking.

"You are *mine!*"

I gurgled – "Fuck you!"

She shook me, there were black dots floating around my vision and I punched her between her breasts. She let go of me and punched me in the face. I dropped and she was on top of me, everything moving too quickly for my mind to follow.

"You are mine!"

I started punching her again, the warping was swallowing the room and the floor we were laying on, struggling for control. Her hands were black talons, but I gripped them when they both came down to strike me in the chest. I started applying pressure, trying to break her bones. Finally, there was a popping from her wrists and she *screamed.*

I kicked her in the groin, getting purchase for my knee, she grunted and I did it several more times, harder each time. She kept that unearthly howl going and I head butted her. It shocked both of us, my vision full of floating stars as I whipped my head forward again. She dogged it, her teeth long needles, darting forward she tried to bite me. I kept kneeing her in the groin and with a surge of strength I threw her from me, her body flipping over the back of the couch. I ran over and started stomping her face. Her eyes were freaking me out; she was just freaking me out.

The inhuman howling suddenly ceased, my bare foot snapped something in her chest. I felt the bone snap under my bare heel. Her rib cage collapsed inwards and I stopped pounding. I was breathing heavy and had sweat pouring out of my pores. Blinking a few times, I realized the fuzzy out of focus effect was gone. I kicked her a few times before it hit me-I had a dead thing in my apartment.

I called the super god knows how long ago. I glanced out of my window; the sun was beginning to rise, the sky a steel blue.

I flopped down next to her (hopefully) dead body and pulled out my phone. I had over thirty missed calls and my text inbox was full. I was confused by this, but I didn't think about too much then. I remember dialing 911, and talking softly to the man who answered at the switchboard. I explained that something attacked me, a woman and I had...

The day was a blur of police, the supervisor, and friends. I had been in my apartment for over four days. It turned out to be a week and the only reason why the police didn't arrive to do a well being check is that when people came by to check on me, I would yell at them through the door.

Ben came over and just sat with me. The paramedics took the body from the apartment with clear horror on their faces when they saw the body. The police and the homicide detective asked lots of questions that I answered truthfully. They eventually left and Ben stayed. He's been my best friend since I moved to the city. He had an interest in the paranormal and occult, and he had some information for me. He had been my research buddy for years, since high school, when the weird shit really started to hit full tilt. Ben knew that something freaky had gone down after I kind of told him what happened over the phone. He called six hours before, and now he was here with some ideas.

"Well, I guess we know what happens when you let a Black Eyed person in. They're mostly kids, and usually come in groups. The few reports of people who let them in usually end in death. It's the kind of people who wouldn't be missed, the type of people that get forgotten or passed over by everyone else they come to, usually at night too. I think they eat souls. You *do* realize there is no apartment across the hall where she was, right?"

"*What?*"

"You should have known something was up when you *just noticed* that she lived there. You look like you've been in a POW camp for months. It's only been seven, eight days since you stopped responding to calls and what not. What *happened* to you?"

"Well, I met Irvina and…"

"I mean to you. What happened in the last week? We should get you to the hospital."

"For what? Anything that happened to me would be emotional, spiritual. Not physical."

"I never thought about that- it being all mental and emotional. Spiritual too. But I was worried about diseases. She looked like a bird."

"Not a bird. Something else, I don't know what the fuck she was. I just want left alone for now."

Ben sat there as I stood, starting the second pack in a row. I never smoked like this, but ever since the homicide detective took my statement, I had been nervous. I was afraid that she was going to somehow leave me in jail for years, the rest of my life. Ben seemed to sense my fears and he cleared his throat before speaking.

"She wasn't human. You're going to be fine. I'll help you as best as I can-" What can I say? Ben was the guy that was there for me when it got crazy, he didn't judge and he did his best to help me figure this shit out. Even that time with the psy-vamp and the beej…not this time though, I wasn't ready to let it go, it felt too personal.

"There's not a damn thing you can do. I need to deal with my own way. I can only make things better by fighting this fight on my own. I'm sorry, Ben, but you need to leave me be for now."

He sat there, frowning until I moved closer to him giving him that look to drive it home, and he understood I meant what

I said. He stood, understanding that I wasn't chasing him out of my life, just out of my apartment for the time being. I walked him to the door and let him out. I could already see the gears turning in his head, the endless catalogue of facts being scrolled through for similarities, possibilities, explanations. Lighting my cigarette I sat down on the couch. I kept thinking of her, of her abilities.

Irvina, what the hell were you?

I frowned at myself, the empty apartment. The answers weren't hiding in the corners, just memories about a girl and the nightmare she really was. Sick of going over it I decided to call work and see if I was fired.

"Power Builders, this is Jenny, how can we build your world today?"

"Um. Jenny this is Jerry. Jerry Stillwell."

"Oh my god! Jerry! Are you ok?" I was more than a little startled to hear the concern in her voice.

"Am I fired? I just need to know if I'm fired."

"Tony is in the office, I'll let you talk to him."

As the line beeped and the call was transferred, I worried.

Tony was a nice guy, but he hated people who didn't show up for work. Granted this was a strange circumstance, and I was hoping he'd have heard what happened to me. I was scared to lose my job, but I waited, holding the phone just a little tighter. Tony's booming voice came on the line, worry evident in it.

"Jerry, where the hell have you *been*?"

"Sick boss, the cops did a well-being check on me. I'm gonna need a few more days. I know it's been a week..."

"Look, son, you're one of my hardest working people. You need a vacation? It's been years since you've had one. I'll give you another week."

"Holy fuck. *Really*?" Tony was nice but he wasn't known for his generosity.

"Yeah son, you deserve it." Pausing a minute to absorb the news I told him the day that I'd be back at work and to my surprise he agreed to it. We said goodbye and I wandered into my bedroom.

Lying on the bed, I stared up at the ceiling, trying to remember what the hell happened. I ran through the last few days and all I could remember is what I've eventually written down here. This is my story and I don't know what the hell I'm going to do. I'm lost on who or what Irvina was and now I have two days before I go back to work.

So, I sit here, not in trouble with the law because they said it wasn't human, but knowing they won't tell me what it was I killed that day. The lead detective came by yesterday and dropped off the autopsy report. He was silent, just handing it to me in the door way. I think he wasn't supposed to share the information, he knew I was confused and scared, but I don't want to think about it. I haven't read the autopsy report, but I know that something is off with all of this.

That's an understatement.

I've been digging around online, researching and reading all the information on the Black Eyed Kid phenomenon. The stories are all similar and beyond freaky. The kids are usually in groups of two, and they have a very monotone vocal pattern. They usually walk up to you in the middle of the night and keep asking over and over to use a phone or for money. The idea is to get past your guard you see, to get into your house and do whatever it is they want to do once they get in there. It isn't until you get angry and tell them to go away that they reveal themselves. Their eyes are pitch black and they get evil when you refuse. Most people have slammed the door shut or run away. The few who did let them in? They died, and the bodies usually looked really fucked up, drained of blood, of vitality. That's what Ben thought

Irvina was and in a way I'd almost like to say he was right.

The deeper I researched in my free time, the more I think she was a Djinn. She was a genie, somehow let loose here in the apartment complex. Or even scarier, she might have always been here. Here in the States we don't get the real story of these things, we get the watered down stuff about wishes and cute cartoons and TV show characters with harem gear on. In the old stories it's a lot more complicated than that. The usual Djinn stories tell of them being territorial, and spiteful of humans, we can't see them, they're supposed to be inter-dimensional beings and sometimes they get reported as shadow people. Sometimes you hear stories of them falling in love and marrying their human lovers. I've come to think that she was drawn here, in a physical form. See, the Djinn are made of smokeless fire, and if she took a human form for me...

She might have fallen in love with me and decided this was the best way of making me love her back. When I saw her true form in the dreams, it angered her. She didn't like me getting past all of her powers, seeing what she really was under it all and decided to kill me or use me for substance. See, a few days after I was found, three floors down they found several people who died too. They looked like they had been burned from the inside out, bones and muscles charred. I have no clue how it could relate to Irvina, but I feel as if it could. I've been researching and there seems to be no indication that she can come back. Once a Djinn has passed away, they're supposed to be gone. That sounds good, like something I might be able to count on.

Trouble is the Djinn were here before us according to mythology and their lineages stretches back for eons. I've got to find all I can about this in case I'm wrong, because if Irvina comes back I don't think she's going to be in love with me anymore. Sometimes at night I see her eyes in my dreams, those eyes and those long black claws and I always wake up in a pool of sweat with my scars screaming.

Block Party

The streets were filled with activity, the heat of the day having faded. I had just pulled into the drive, and I stared up and down the street. The Wilders chased each other in the front lawn with Super Soakers, Anna squealed wildly as Timothy sprayed her across the back. They were a couple of game journalists that moved in several months ago. They were usually the first to pop over and talk when Veronica and I were sitting on the porch. She usually sipped a tea, while I smoked and maybe had a Smirnoff Ice. They'd sit and talk for a few hours, the sun setting behind the house before we went our ways. Timothy had seen some of the stuff I had been working on in my office; he worked a floor above me. It was funny, me working on game design and my neighbor being a game journalist.

Jim and his wife were out for the week, but they left their car in the driveway to make it look like they were home. I kept an eye out on their house, but this street was quiet. Tonight, however, it was going to get loud. Some friends cleared a street party with the city, and they'd set up saw horses at both ends of the street to keep people out. I smelled the steaks and burgers cooking three houses down. To the south, the DJ arrived in his beat up van. I knew of him from several parties that work had thrown, and he was good. To the north, past the house with the grilling meat, the kids of the street were in the front lawn, a movie played for them on an inflatable screen.

I looked toward our doorway and Veronica stood there, her hip against the frame. Her arms were crossed, but she gestured with her pointer finger for me to come up. I closed the car door and locked it as I walked up the four steps to the covered porch.

"Hey baby, you doing ok?"

Veronica uncrossed her arms and wrapped them around my waist, hands gripping my ass.

"We have maybe twenty minutes before the food is ready," she whispered in my ear. I jumped when she squeezed my ass harder.

She led me upstairs, shedding clothes every five or six feet. By the time we reached the bedroom she was nude and bent over the bed. As I spread her legs apart, I kneeled behind her, licked her outer folds. She pressed herself harder against my face, and I started licking her sweet spot. She reached behind her, wanting to grab my hair. She couldn't reach, so she pulled away as she sat on the edge of the bed. She spread her legs, leaned back a little. I got between her legs, hands on her thighs as she spread herself open for me. I moved in close, on my knees on the carpeted floor. Her scent filled my nostrils, her arousal evident. I licked her sweet spot in a circular motion and she gasped in pleasure. As her pleasure rode upwards, I switched directions. My tongue pressed against her clit, and we moaned in pleasure. Suddenly, her hands were buried in my hair and I started moaning louder as she pushed me into her groin.

She came hard, her moans loud and insistent. She pushed me back with a firm hand on my chest, as she was in the center of the bed, Veronica opened her folds. Turned to the right, she looked at me. I dropped my pants and boxers and climbed on the bed.

My hands gripped her hips as I slipped inside her. She started to thrust backward, her face buried in the pillows. She moaned as she lifted her head, and put her hands on the headboard for better stability. She gripped the top, still as can be while she tried to hold her orgasm until I came. I was moaning for both of us, loud and hard. My hands went to her breasts, squeezed and pinched her nipples. She turned her face to me, teeth clenched.

"Jules, come! I can't hold off anymore!"

I allowed myself to give in, rocked forward and back as it built, and then I came. My wife unleashed a scream from the bottom of her soul. My hands were on her hips again while she leaned against me and thrust back to meet me. We slid backwards, moaned louder as a second orgasm ripped through us.

She thrust faster, turned her face towards mine as she rode it into the next. She kissed me fiercely, her moans turned to whimpers of pleasure. We slowed down our pace, a gentle and loving motion. As we slowed even more, we gasped for air between kisses and then we were stretched on the bed, her atop me. I nuzzled her neck for a few minutes as we lay there, getting our wind and minds back.

When I looked at the clock, it was about time for the DJ and food to be ready. She slid off of me, and hopped into the shower real quick. I grabbed some clothes for both us and I got dressed. I left hers on the bed, and I went down the stairs. As I picked up her discarded clothes, I started laughing to myself. It was a full laugh, from the bottom of my stomach, and I almost sounded crazy. The sound of my laughter made me laugh even harder, and the feeling of my drying cock against my boxers made me laugh more. It's this tick I have, it happens when I'm left too sensitive afterwards. Sometimes Veronica made a point of teasing me to hear it. I stopped at the bottom of the stairs and I took a few deep breaths. I had it under some control, only a laugh here and there. I walked back up the stairs, still laughing. I'm not sure where it came from, maybe it wasn't just the sensitivity.

Veronica stood, half dressed in the bedroom, when I came in laughing."Jules, what's so funny? You ok?"

I caught a breath and the strange laughter folded into chuckles.

"Yeah, honey, I just got the giggles. That was hot, thank you."

She threw me a sideways glance and smiled.

"You sure you're ok?"

I took a deep breath and nodded once. Then I put her clothes in the hamper and reached out for her hand. We walked down the stairs hand in hand, I led the way. We got onto our porch the moment the music started. It was an '80s tune that I love, and I hummed along as we went up the sidewalk.

Still humming to myself, dancing a little too, we made our way up the Jones' driveway. The newlywed couple decided to throw this party for us, and the pair made out as they flipped steaks and put cheese on the burgers.

The street was full of people; most of them seated at the picnic tables. The Wilders came up behind us, still soaked from the water gun fight.

"Hey, guys, can I get a steak and a burger?"

Sven handed me a sturdy paper plate and plopped a steak on it. I turned a little, towards James, and he plopped a burger on the plate. I scooted over and Veronica got the same thing while I made my burger.

She had her burger built when I grabbed us a couple cans of pop, balancing them in one hand as I carried my plate with the other. We sat at the only empty table and the Wilders joined us.

"When're you guys coming by the office again for a preview of the beta build, Timothy?"

"I think me and Anna are gonna pop over on Tuesday, if Tom doesn't have anything for us. You going to be there?"

"I should be, I've been working on the scripting for a few days now, and I think the new missions will bring the change to the story we've needed. You know that Fanny has been trying to work on the story for a few months since Harold died and couldn't do the voice over work."

Timothy nodded and buried himself in his food. Anna and Veronica talked about a TV show they watched, so I decided to follow suit, and bit a good-sized mouthful out of my burger. Sven and his husband finally sat down, the music throbbed at the other end of the street. The bass traveled along the pavement and my feet twitched. Sven sat next to me, while James sat across from him.

"Holy crap, James, this is fucking good!"

"It's how we do it at the restaurant. Season the steaks over night in apple cider vinegar and Montreal steak seasoning. Cook 'em on the grill to order."

"That simple?"

James nodded and dug into his steak.

Steak sauce and juices ran down his clean-shaven face. I wanted to reach out and wipe it away, but I didn't, it would have looked weird to people. Sven and James teased each other about who had the best meat, jokes that were normal to us who knew them. They ran a restaurant together and had faced some bad times when people realized they were a couple, but once people realized it didn't matter and how good the food was, their business began booming.

He and James kept giving each other the eye, like Veronica had done with me earlier. I finished my burger, trying not to chuckle at them. I found Sven cute; his office worker looks drove me nuts. Timothy did too sometimes ,when he was dressed up. Seeing either of them in a dress shirt and tie made my heart leap. I stood up, and looked for more burgers. I should have been full from the previous steak and burger, but I skipped lunch so I could eat tonight. I picked up two burgers and passed on the buns, then grabbed a plastic fork and headed back to the table.

Sven and James played with each other's feet under the table, and Timothy joked with James about something when I came back. The three guys were talking about how to make a great salmon steak, so I asked Veronica if she wanted more.

"More what?" She batted her eyes at me for a moment, teasing me.

"Steak or pop."

She just chuckled and stood.

"I'm good for now, hon. You must be starving."

I sat down with a nod, dug into the thick burgers, and looked at everyone on the street. I smiled, thinking that things were good. Veronica and Anna danced to the music as they moved down the street. Veronica wiggled her butt as she walked, while Anna laughed as they had to swerve around people and talked to other people as they walked. As I finished up my burgers, I stood up. Having gathered the plates from everyone at the table, I walked to the trash can on the corner. The sun was had started setting behind our houses and the chill creeped in a little.

I blinked, watched everything around me change. In a moment, I see everyone as skeletons and the houses overrun with greenery. I jumped a little, as I've never had that vivid of a day dream before. Veronica and Anna slow danced to a song, the people that surrounded them were too. The music is louder than before and the skeletons seemed to be living and having a merry time. Several times a day in the past I would have these day dreams that seemed to overtake my senses, to change the scents or sights I should have been seeing into alien landscapes. The doctors said its fine, normal even, but it happened. This lasted longer than normal, and I must have looked panicked.

I started to blink rapidly for a few seconds, scared.

"Jules! You ok, man?"

Timothy had my arm and he shook me. I openned my eyes and stared at him. I expected empty sockets and a skeleton asking me questions, but it's him. I jumped again, heart racing a steady beat. I nodded once, twice.

"Yeah. I'm ok. It's been a long week apparently."

"Yeah, I have to go to Tokyo next week and Anna has to stay here. She's bummed out about it, but hey, I gotta go. The conference is going on and if they don't send me, a freelancer is just going to fuck it up."

I nodded, his hand still on my arm. I turned and looked at him, his eyes boring into mine. He tugs once, in the direction of his house. I nodded once, almost imperceptibly.

He let go of my arm and we looked at our wives. They danced with each other, lost in the music and the movements. I followed him as he chattered about the new computer he'd built. I played along and followed him into his garage. I'd been staring at his ass in those jeans, with each step the muscles of his ass pulled and moved like liquid under the fabric. He worked out in the gym downstairs. My frame had always been towards slim. I'm about six feet tall and my hair is a dark black with grey along the sides. I'm only in my early thirties, but the grey appeared in college. I loved how it made me look, so I didn't fret over it.

We were in the kitchen when Timothy turned and faced me. He dropped to his knees, surprising me. He had my belt undone and my pants half off of me when I started to pull down my boxers a bit. My cock sprung free and hit his chin. He chuckled as he looked up at me. His three day beard and shiny eyes shocked me, he was so handsome.

He took me as deep as he could into his mouth, started a slow bob. As his lips slid up and down my shaft, my hands went to his hair. I moaned lightly, half scared that Veronica or Anna will find us. I started to thrust, the blowjob too much to handle. He stopped bobbing and let me thrust. I stiffened and came once. He swallowed it, looking up at me as he did.

I let go of his hair and his head and, before I pulled up my boxers and pants, I helped him stand. He leaned against my chest and I smelled his hair. His brown, close cut hair smelled of an exotic fruit. My hands went to his lower back and I hugged him.

He pulled away from my chest and stared at me. There was a fear in his eyes, of losing me, of losing Anna. I kissed his forehead and he hugged me tight. His frame was warm against me and it felt good.

Seated in the recliner, I heard Veronica calling for me. I slowly remembered coming in to play games with Timothy, and sitting here. I must have eaten too much and gotten sleepy.

"Jules! Honey, wake up. Its bedtime, let's go."

I jumped awake and Veronica was seated on the couch next to me, shaking my leg. I looked around the room groggily. Timothy turned off his TV and I noticed the controller in my hand. I stood up on wobbly legs and handed the controller to Timothy.

"Holy crap, did I fall asleep? What time is it?"

I'd left my cell phone in the car when I got home, but I patted my pockets for it anyway. I looked around for a clock, and on the wall the digital one glowed in the low lights. I saw that it was 11:30, and I was confused. My pants were on, and I –

"Ah fuck, it was a dream."

"What was a dream, hon? Let's get you home. How many pops did you have?"

"One or two. You think my sugar went out of whack?"

"You fell asleep an hour after you got here, Timothy was just saying. He kept an eye on you. Me and Anna had fun dancing –"

"Oh hell! The block party!"

Veronica held my hand as she led me out the door, that is, until I planted my feet. I turned and looked at Timothy, he had a strange look in his eyes. He kept staring at Veronica and Anna, who was sitting in the recliner, checking her phone.

"Veronica, Jules, you two have a good night." She looked up at us, smiling. I half waved and Veronica echoed it back to her.

We got on the porch and I turned and looked at Veronica. She was beautiful in the dark, her white skin shone in the moonlight, her long red hair framed her face perfectly and her tank top showed her curves. I hadn't forgotten how beautiful she was, but I got caught off guard by her sometimes. I breathed deep and leaned in for a kiss. She kissed me back, tasting and smelling of a grain alcohol. She giggled and I nipped at her neck.

"Somebody had a few drinks, eh?"

"Three or four. I'm good."

Her cheeks were a light red and I realized that she was a bit tipsy. We walked to the sidewalk, both of us looking inebriated. I was groggy from the sugar and she was tipsy. The music had been turned down to a much lower volume, and people were still seated, drinking at the picnic tables. We waved goodnight to people and stumbled home. We got upstairs after that and passed out in each other's arms.

Chapter 2

I woke up as the sunlight streamed into my eyes the next morning. I rolled over towards Veronica's side of the bed and found that it was empty. I lay there and listened for her. She was downstairs, rattling around doing something.

Eyes closed, I thought back to the blowjob Timothy gave me. It felt real; it felt like it happened, but from what I could tell I hadn't gotten one from him. I was bi, but I never slept with Timothy. Hell, after college, I found Veronica and fell in love. We got married three years after we met and now here we were. I sat up, careful to avoid the sunlight in my eyes, and then I stood and went to the bathroom. Dressed for the day in yesterday's clothes, I knew it must have been a dream.

I went downstairs to find Veronica had made coffee and toast for us. She turned and smiled, humming a song to herself as she poured the coffee. I sat down at the table, amused by her.

As she flitted across the kitchen, grabbing butter and cinnamon for the toast, I noticed she was just wearing a long t-shirt with no underwear.

"Veronica?"

"Yeah, honey?"

"Why are you naked under that shirt?"

She turned and leaned against the counter. She had a jar of jelly in her hands, and she smiled at me.

"You'll see. Eat, wake up. We have a long day ahead of us."

I walked over to her and kissed her deep when I reached her. I snaked my hand to her hip, and tried to get under the shirt. Her hand slapped mine before I could see it. I snapped my hand away and rubbed it.

"Sit down, *now*. You are to eat and wake up."

I jumped at her commands and, I obeyed. Once seated, I stared at her, trying to see a glimpse of her ass or a little more as she finished the food. She put the breakfast on the table and I was careful not to touch her. That slap hurt and I was a bit embarrassed. She sat down across from me, and demanded my attention with a glance.

"Eyes on your food."

I blinked and stared into her eyes as she pulled the shirt off. She was seated in the sunlight, nude. I snapped my eyes to my food and I started eating. I felt myself stirring, my arousal more emotional and mental at this stage. I struggled not to look up at her bare breasts as they swayed as she ate. In a few minutes I was done and I snapped my eyes to hers.

She smiled and that glint I love flared in her eyes. I swallowed, fighting the urge to look at her breasts. I clearly struggled and she giggled, her smile taking my attention.

I started giggling too and she looked down. I did too, but I snapped my eyes upwards before she noticed.

"Look at them, it's ok. I'm impressed, actually. You've never been able to do that for long."

I sat there, having suddenly remembered Timothy going down

on me. My eyes must have twitched funny or something, because she noticed something had shifted.

"What, baby? You ok?"

I nodded as I stared at her chest. Her brown nipples were dark and they stuck out an inch and a half. I loved playing with them, a nice firm feeling when they were in my hands or mouth. She circled her pointer fingers around the areolas and shivered.

She got to her feet and walked around to my side of the table. We started kissing, deep and passionate kisses that made my heart swell, hers too. She pulled back and stared into my eyes. I smiled, honest and deep. Her hands went to my crotch and through my boxers she felt my half hard cock.

The glint was back and she had me stand up. I stood and she pulled off my boxers as I stepped out of them. My cock was free and she led me to the couch. She sat down on it and had me kneel in front her. I put my hands behind my back and I settled in. I wasn't sure what she planned on doing, but I was curious. She picked up her cell phone from the stand next to her, the tapping of her fingernails loud in the quiet.

She sat there, nude, as she checked her emails and messages online. I was patient, and after a half hour she asked if I need to reposition. I shook my head and she went back to her phone. Her glances were more frequent, but I have my eyes in a soft focus. I was waiting to see what would happen when she stood up. As she flopped her phone on the couch, she sat up with instructions for me.

"Stand up. Turn around. Kneel again. Hands behind your back."

I listened to her instructions and followed them. I stood and turned away from her. Then I knelt down and scooted closer to her by a few inches. I heard her as she rummaged in the drawer on the stand. Before I knew it I had a blindfold on me, knotted tight and I couldn't see anything. My hands were expertly rigged in comfortable rope handcuffs. My breathing picked up pace, deeper as I sensed my arousal rising. Behind the blindfold my eyes were open and I felt my pupils dilate. My breath was suddenly much deeper and then it was slower, the adrenaline spike subsided. I felt my heart rate as it slowed by a few beats. I slipped into my comfort zone, where I needed to be for us to enjoy ourselves. I relaxed, my muscles loosened. I felt them give into the binds, like my soul had been set free in them.

In the blindfold and rope handcuffs, *I am free*. My soul was released from the constrictions of my daily life. When Veronica dominated me, I was free. Sometimes I have to be tied and controlled to lose control. In my office job, I have to be in control of the uncontrollable, to fix the impossible. When I give into to Veronica, when I allow control to be taken from me I am released. We didn't do this often, this was something special.

Yes, we were both bi and she was my dominant. While it is sometimes unusual for men to be submissive, I am. Her hands started caressing my neck, my shoulders. Her warm hands slipped from me and suddenly I had her nails digging into my ass cheeks. I jumped and she dug in deeper. I hissed through clenched teeth as she relaxed her fingers, ten she ran her fingernails from my ass cheeks to my hips. From my hips the thin nails slid upwards. I started to twitch and fought the urge to do so. Her fingers clamped around my nipples as they squeezed and twisted into the right pressure. I needed more and I was unashamed to admit it.

"Harder. Oh god, harder."

I moaned in pleasure when she reached the right pressure and I sunk into myself a bit more. A few seconds passed and her right hand snaked itself to my hip, then my ass cheek. She sunk her nails in, less rough this time and I moaned in pleasure. Her short nails retracted from my flesh and her middle finger started massaging my asshole. I felt myself open and her finger slipped in, pressed and thrust slowly and gently. I relaxed, leaned into her, and then her grip on my nipple was gone. My eyes were closed behind the blindfold and her hand wrapped around my hard on. She stroked me softly as she thrust her finger two knuckles deep into me. I moaned loudly and exposed my neck.

Her teeth clamped down onto my shoulder, the pressure erotic. I felt myself as I dived into the slight stupor that good dominant sex brought me. I wiggled my fingers a little to see what she'd do. Surprisingly, she kneeled closer and her breasts rested in my hands. She moved back a little, and I pinched her nipples. I hear her sigh in pleasure and I started playing with them right. She stroked and thrust to a rhythm now and my fingers got into it too.

I rocked against the air and in her tight fist I came, sprayed all over the carpet and her hand, but she stroked me more. I wanted to pull away, my flesh too sensitive down there. She started stroking faster, her finger deep in my ass. She tapped something just right inside me and I came for a second time. I felt my come spraying out, the veins carrying it bulged with the amount of it.

Veronica pulled back, her nipples freed from my hands and her finger slipped out of me. Her left hand wiped my come onto a towel or something she had hidden under the couch for this. Lying headfirst on the floor as I panted, the orgasms drained me of energy. As I lay there, she undid the rope handcuffs and my hands were mine again. I stretched out on the carpet, eyes still covered. Her hands were on my back, rubbing and stroking circulation back into me and I began to drift to sleep, safe and at peace.

I woke up some time later and she stood over me. I looked up and she had a strap on bouncing in front of me. I smiled, and her eyes and laugh told me all I needed to know. It's a decently lengthened one, about seven long and about two thick. I reached up and started stroking it like it was a real cock. Once I slipped up to my knees, I started to take it in my mouth, her hands in my hair. I took it in, a few inches at a time. Eventually I had it all the way in, only a few inches left on the rig. I moaned softly when I pulled back, and Veronica's hands were clinging to my neck and shoulders. She resisted the urge to pull me deeper and I could tell it was difficult.

She pulled away and pushed me to the floor; I lifted my legs as soon as I was settled. She draped them over her shoulders, then she slipped a condom on the toy and soon it was inside me. I gasped, the pleasure of being filled a rare one. She pounded into me; my hands held my cheeks apart and needed something to grip. I threw my head back as my eyes rolled backwards from the pleasure. The strokes were hard and fast, just how I wanted them. My cock was hard and she stroked it again. I looked at her and her eyes were wide open, stared at me in delight. My come splashed across her stomach, not as much as before. She kept pounding me.

"Veronica, come baby. Please, come for me?"

"Little bit longer, I'm almost there."

Her back arched, and we froze. The orgasm rolled through her hard and her body shuddered with the strength of it. She pumped her hips a few more times, small short strokes. The two-way in her was close to making her come again and she wanted to savor it. My hands went to her hips, my legs and feet pressed against her upper chest now. She thrust like that for a few minutes and then slipped out of me.

She undid the harness for the strap on, slipped it from her and set it on the couch. She reached for me and I sit up, taking her hands. She kissed me, deep and repeatedly for several minutes while I worked myself hard again. We were both coated in sweat and breathing heavily, unable to calm down until we got off again. I sat on the couch and pulled her to me. My cock was hard again, so she turned around and lowered herself onto me.

My cock slipped into her hot, drenched slit, hands on her hips, thebslid over her breasts and shoulders. I thrust upwards, right hand fingering her clit as I thrust, left arm wrapped around her waist. She started to thrust back in time with me and, before I knew it, she leaned back into me and kissed me. She came again, her pussy clinched tight around me as her orgasm rolled through her. Her neck and cheek were smothered in kisses as she came down from the orgasm. I continued to thrust up into her, I was close to coming too. Her silence was broken and she whispered to me.

"Come, baby, one last time, come. Please?"

My hands were on her hips when I came, frozen in place, we both felt it as it spurted into her. Almost as suddenly as the orgasm came to me, it was gone. The heat on my cheeks and chest faded quickly, my cock softened. She stood slowly, pulled me out of her. As we laid there, under the throw blanket on the couch, I realized it wasn't even noon yet.

***

We were driving back from grocery shopping and the sun was going down. I was driving and Veronica had her hand on my thigh as I drove. She squeezed off and on and I knew she wanted to say something.

"Veronica, just say it. This isn't like you, to not say it."

"Jules, it's kind of weird to talk about. I *want to*, but..."

"Is it Anna?"

"No, it's more than just her. I haven't cheated!"

"Veronica, I know you haven't. You would've said something by now, you can't keep secrets that easily."

"You want to go to the club?"

I tapped the brake and glanced at her.

"*That* club?"

"Yeah."

I kept on driving as I thought to myself. I wasn't mad, just shocked. It had been years since we went to Ziggy's, an alternative sex club. I glanced at the clock in the car and then at Veronica. She stared ahead, her hand still on my thigh. I could tell that it was really difficult for her to bring this up. I wondered if she and Anna had gotten close to something and she backed off because of our marriage.

"Did something happen? *Why now*? It's been *years* since we went there, much less anything else. I'm not scared or worried, just curious."

"I – *need* to go. You do too. You've been thinking of Timothy. I know you have."

"Talking in my sleep again?"

"Yeah," she whispered. She was running numbers in her head again, like she did years ago. Playing with different outcomes and what not. We all do it, straight, bi or whatever. We run numbers in our heads, try to sort out the statistics of what would happen, how it could. It doesn't mean you're a bad person, just means that there are possibilities, potential changes that might be worth the risk.

"Let's get the food home and we'll get ready."

She turned and looked at me and I glanced at her as I nodded several times. She leaned closer, her head on my shoulder. Taking my right hand from the wheel, I wrapped it around her shoulder.

***

We pulled into the parking lot, and saw that it was packed. The back parking lot was always the first to fill up. We climbed out of the car.

Veronica was wearing a green satin dress that ended just below her lower ass, when she moved the right way anyone watching could see the round curves of her cheeks. I was in a dress shirt and pants, all black. We walked hand in hand to the front door, and I noticed a man who stood across the street, trying to hide in a shadow. He was tall and had a potbelly that gave him away. He leaned out to look at us, and his bug eyes burned into my memory. They were a steel grey that pierced the night and bored straight into me. I looked at him and he moved back into the shadows, afraid that he had been seen.

We kept on going, Veronica not seeing him, so I didn't bring it up.

We stepped in, and, as we paid the cover charge, the music hit us. The double doors buzzed open and we walked in. A handsome man and his lover in an orange top snuggled as they walked to the exit. Veronica turned to me and smiled, taking my hand. I unbuttoned my shirt at the neck and exposed my collar. It was a thin metal collar with a padlock on the front. If the padlock wasn't attached it would have looked like any other interesting necklace that was tight against my neck, but it got more interesting with the padlock.

On Veronica's left hand there was a thick bracelet, and that had a key on it. Her right wrist had a glow bracelet. We walked past the tables of people as they drank and screamed over the music to talk. We decided to go right to the dance floor. She took me by the hand, led me.

We were on the dance floor and I couldn't dance. I ended up just throwing myself around, getting lost in the people surrounding us. The bodies pressed against us, the industrial music loud and crisp. The bass shook your bones, and my ribcage felt like it was rattled to pieces. I closed my eyes and just moved. Veronica moved with a grace I hadn't seen in awhile when I opened my eyes. She pressed herself against a couple that surrounded her. I felt my breath catch in my throat, my heart pounded from excitement. She squeezed past them and moved to me, her hands ran down my face, and then she gripped the padlock with her left hand.

She pulled me down to her, which wasn't very far, but it was the intensity of the moment that made all the difference. What she did next made me jump, my body tensed and relaxed in milliseconds. She gave me a deep kiss, and, while she was kissed me, distracted me, her other hand undid my padlock. I pulled back as I jumped in shock. Our eyes were locked on each others' in the flashing neon stage lights. She had a twinkle in her eye as she pulled me close to her.

"Find a man, for you."

I pulled back, looked at her in surprise. She smiled wickedly, an erotic edge to her features suddenly. She was hot when she was getting dressed and she was even hotter now. I didn't know what the hell was going on, but I leaned into her ear.

"Are you looking for a woman?"

She nodded and yelled back a reply.

"I got us a room in the suites, it'll fit four fine!"

I pulled back, looked around me at the men that I could see. There were handsome men, normal guys, and everything in between. In Ziggy's the color band they gave you after you paid told everyone your orientation if you set it up before hand. One of the reasons why Ziggy was still around is because it embraced the internet in the late 90s to get people together for what they wanted, needed. Veronica and I discovered it in college, just like our dominant and submissive roles in our relationship.

We came here often, to use the rooms so we wouldn't get caught in awkward situations in the dorms. The rooms were cleaned by staff the moment the keycard was returned, and with the black lights in the room, you could tell they were cleaned as deeply as they could be. Veronica had already gotten a room. She must have planned this for awhile. Our bands glowed in the dark, then the light dulled them, the dark. They were glow bracelets, giving us access to everywhere clients could go.

"What room number?"

"319. Meet me there in an hour or so, man in tow or not."

I nodded silently, and she disappeared into the throng of dancers on the floor. I could see glimpses of her green dress, and I decided to go up to the second floor, to see if I could focus on a guy or two up there. I was sweating, my shirt soaked, hair drenched. It was hot in here, the people who brushed into me were just as sweaty, but it was more than the heat. I was light-headed from just the thought of possibly being with a man. Touching, feeling, and tasting someone; some *guy*.

I hadn't felt the touch of a man in years, and somehow Veronica knew I had been having thoughts of Timothy. As erotic as it was, it also sent a shiver of fear through me, caused me to hesitate as I looked at the men in the club, tried to gauge who would be worth the risk. I felt guilty and yet, at the same time, I knew she and Anna were becoming more than just friends and I knew I was fine with it. She needed that interaction, I knew she did. For a moment I was consumed by the back and forth, the taboo that was our lives, but then those thoughts were pushed to the side and my heart pounded as I ran up the stairs. I got up there and went to a vending machine. I dropped money on a bottle of water, not caring about the price, then I walked over to the railing, scanned everywhere for a man who was my type.

I loved men who were muscular in a lithe and natural way. No bears, cubs, or otters for me. I wanted a man with muscle and strength to dominate. I was a switch, and the fact that I could switch, maybe tonight, made my head spin harder. I downed the bottle in three or four gulps and set the empty on the table next to me.

I looked down to see Veronica was in the middle of the floor, her graceful moves got attention from everyone. Hands caressed her, touched her. My cock got hard as I watched, and breathed faster. I saw a man reach out and cup her left breast from behind, her hands ran down the front of a redhead. The redhead was dressed in a leather crop-top, her breasts hung free. Veronica stroked her nipples as more hands touched and probed her.

Then something strange occurred. I felt a hand on my hip, and another on my belt. I looked down at the hands, they were male. I wiggled my ass a little and the belt was undone just enough to enable a hand to reach in. It wrapped itself around me, absorbing the body heat coming off of me in waves. The cool hand felt good and the kisses on my neck were even better. The stubble scratched a little, but I didn't care. The other hand crept to my shirt, pinched my nipple as I was stroked. On the floor, Veronica was lost in the crowd again and I closed my eyes. The soft skin wrapped around my cock, stroked it perfectly in time with what I needed, it was amazing.

"She's fucking hot, isn't she?" Timothy said loudly.

I stiffened, stood straight up and yanked his hand from my pants.

As I spun around, I could feel my heart stop, I turned to see his face was right there. We were less than a foot apart, face to face.

"Holy fuck!"

His eyes got wide when he realized who he had been stroking off. I glanced at his wrist, and I was shocked to see his bracelet was the same shade and color as mine. I put my belt back together and turned to look at the dance floor again. Anna and Veronica were dancing together, close and erotic. Between rubbing against themselves and the people surrounding them, they traded kisses. I turned back to Timothy.

I raised my wrist in question and he nodded. I beckoned him closer, put my hands on his ass and leaned into his ear.

"You sure? Do you want to do something with me?"

I glanced at him, his face, and it told me all I needed to know. His eyes blinked rapidly as he nodded, and I started undoing the belt in his jeans. He leaned back to look at me as I moved. The music now overcame all my senses except for touch. My eyes were locked onto his, but I could barely see through the tears suddenly welling there. He reached out, using both thumbs to wipe them away. He smiled softly and then he put my hand in his pants, pressed himself against me.

I started to cup his balls, squeezed and felt them in my hand. I felt him growing harder as the seconds went by and I let him out. Stroking him with my palm, where I could catch his orgasm, I mimicked the same strokes and speed he used on me. In the loud music he didn't care about people hearing him and he was almost screaming as he came into my palm. With my free left hand, I reached for a napkin on the table.

Ziggy's is strange, because you can walk in and see all kinds of things going on. They had bondage art shows several times a year where performers would put on displays and live acts. Most of the time there were people in various stages of dress and undress. All of it was accepted here, unless of course, it was illegal. Me stroking off Timothy and pocketing the napkin, was normal, really normal for here. I slipped him back into his boxers, and redid his jeans.

"We have a room! Let's get the ladies."

He shook his head, "No. I want you to fuck me. I want you bad."

Our eyes locked and I felt the world tilt again. I glanced at the floor below and Veronica and Anna sitting at a table, side by side.

"Veronica has the key! We gotta get it from her first!"

"I have a room too, we can just go!"

I glanced at my watch and only a half hour had passed. We had time before Veronica wanted to meet me at the room. I followed Timothy through the throng of people, his ass hugged by the jeans. His tight t-shirt showed off his muscles as he was pushing through the crowd. I wanted him, and bad, but I kept my cool. We got to the stairwell that led up to the suites and three guys came down in a hand holding knot. I smiled, I thought that they all looked cute together. Timothy led me up-stairs, to his room. It was 215, a floor below ours. He slipped in and I fol-lowed. Once the door was shut, we undressed.

He pulled his shirt off, facing away from me. His back was strong and muscular, it turned me on to watch it move, and then he turned to undo his belt. His pectorals and stomach were erotic, almost hairless and I needed to touch him. I walked over to him, my hands ran over his chest, back, and shoulders. He shuddered slightly at my touch and I pulled him close to me. I kissed him gently on the cheek, then the lips. We embraced and he undid the buttons on my shirt as I dropped it. Our bodies were pressed together, my hands on his ass as he wrapped his arms around my waist. We kissed and touched as we moved to the bed in the middle of the room, a large one. The California King was big and strong enough to hold many people. I pulled from his embrace and sank to the floor.

As I undid his jeans I had him pull his shoes and pants off. The boxers were next to go, and then he was nude. I took his half hard dick in my hand and stroked him to full erection. My lips wrapped around him and I took him in as deep as I could. I bobbed quickly on him and I listened as he started moaning loudly, his hands in my hair. He started to pump his hips as the pleasure took over and he gripped my hair tighter.

As the pumping and gripping increased, my hands snaked to his ass and I slipped in the first knuckle on my middle finger. I spread his legs apart and he allowed me to enter him a little bit more. There was a sudden jerking motion and then he came in my mouth. He had six or seven huge spurts of come and I swallowed it as fast as I could so I could keep breath-ing. I pulled my lips and mouth from him, licked the shaft as I did so. His dick was a good seven inches long, and I was kissing the head of it when he spurted a little on my lips.

I found this hot as fuck, as I stood to start kissing him, he licked his come from my lips first. My hands ended up on his shoulders and after a few minutes of this, I spun him around. I pushed him to the bed and he climbed up on it. His naked body tensed as he got into the bottom position, on his knees and leaning forward. His head was buried in his arms, but I rested my hand on his left hip.

He turned to look at me, and I motioned for him to roll over. He did and I took off my pants and boxers. My shoes had come off when we walked into the room, and my clothes were scattered like his. My watch told me that it was almost time to meet Veronica, but I needed him. No, it was more than need; I had to have him in that moment.

Getting myself hard, I lifted his legs, placed them on my shoulders. He was open out of anticipation of this, of me. The table next to the bed had condoms, and he threw one at my chest. I caught it and slipped it on. In seconds I was easing myself into him.

I started slowly; my strokes measured and long. Soon, I was deep in him and I felt his tightness give some. He relaxed, and stared at me while he bit his lip. The bass from the music was throbbed through the floors as I began to thrust, hard.

My hands were wrapped around his calves and shins as I fucked him. His moans were pure and primal, the sensations going through us were primal. I started to bite his calves, his cock hard and standing up. He reached down and started stroking it, pointing it at me. My eyes closed, clenched shut, and soon the sensation of having Timothy open to me was more than I could handle. I came inside him, and seconds after the pulse of my cock sent him the signal that I'd come, he splashed my stomach in hot come.

The door creaked open, and Veronica and Anna kissed as they undressed each other on their way to the bed. They were unaware of us, passion and need carried them through the room. Timothy was frozen, eyes wide with fear and arousal. He looked at me, then my wife, then his. My eyes locked on him. He nodded slightly as I slipped from him.

I scooted over, slid the condom off and into the trash next to the bed. Our wives kissed and touched, lost in arousal and awakening. I stared at the women, Timothy and I both just watched. They saw us, and we scooted from the bed. It was not with a voyeuristic intent; we were actually intrigued by the intimacy of the women. They were nude on the bed, stretched out side by side. Anna had her left leg between Veronica's and their hands caressed each other. Veronica ran her fingertips over Anna's back, but if you looked closely her fingers were barely above her skin. As she ran her fingertips down her lover's spine, Anna twitched and moaned. Her hands slipped to Veronica's face, cupping her cheeks as they kissed. I could feel a heat coming from the ladies as they explored each other. Anna straddled my wife suddenly, her hands running down her neck, sides, hips. She lifted her hands and, using the lightest touch of her palms, aroused Veronica's nipples to full stiffness. I heard her gasp in pleasure as the barest touch sent shockwaves through her.

I sat down on a chair, a plastic one set to the side. My eyes took in everything in the room in front of me. I've made love to my wife, taken hours to get her aroused and ready to make love, but this intimacy was different. It was a deeper one and it made me understand her need for a woman.

Anna leaned over my wife, kissed her, and they had their hands clasped together, fingers intertwined tightly. Veronica turned towards me once and our eyes locked. I silently told her I understood, because I did. Timothy and I sat there, in hushed awe. I knew I wasn't aroused physically, but emotionally by seeing my wife being fulfilled by a connection she *needed*. I knew that if nothing else, Veronica had what she desired and ached to have for a long time. Even if it was for just a night, she was fulfilled.

Veronica moaned softly. As I looked at her and sent her my thoughts, Anna moved between her legs. Veronica turned her head and looked down at her lover. Anna licked and bit her thighs as she moved lower. My wife's hands were buried in the thick hair between her legs as she writhed for a few moments and then moaned as she came. Anna giggled as she pushed Veronica's thighs apart, so she could scoot up and kiss my wife from tummy to lips, their hands caressed and touched. Anna gasped, sharp and quick. I watched as she started to lick and bite Veronica's neck and her gasps matched Anna's.

Before I know it, Veronica had her face buried between Anna's legs, from under her. Anna whipped her head back and forth, her legs trembled with the stress of not wanting to fall or come. I watched my wife as her hands explored and stroked an orgasm from Anna. She came, looked over at us, but not truly seeing us. I glanced over at Timothy and he was in the same state as me, emotionally and mentally aroused. I reached my hand over to his leg, squeezed once. He patted my hand, held it with his.

The ladies were lying side by side as they stroked smaller, more intimate orgasms as they kissed and whispered things to each other. I turned my palm up and Timothy gripped my hand tighter than before. I glanced over at him and there was this understanding, this knowledge that this was something we'd needed for a long time. I didn't know what to say, so I didn't say anything.

Our wives noticed us sitting still, absorbed in the room, silent. Our hands were still gripped tight, and they beckoned us over to them. I walked over towards Veronica and she sat on the edge of the bed. Her eyes locked on mine as we smiled shyly at the same time. Her face went into domme mode, a sly grin and mischievous look in her eyes. I scooted closer and she reached out.

She took my cock in her hand, stroked me hard. I was stiff and wanted to do something, anything to make her happy. I scooted even closer, her lips brushing my tip. Timothy climbed behind his wife and she made small murmuring noises as he ran his hands over her body, touched and pleased.

Veronica took me in her mouth, bobbed slowly as she moaned. Anna had made her come at least twice now and she had a dazed look in her eyes. Veronica bobbed faster, eyes locked on mine. As my hands caressed her hair and jaw line, I came hard. I clenched my eyes shut and pulled from her when she let go of me. I sank onto my legs, I shook. It was the shaking of a good orgasm or love making. You could feel the muscles relax, the tension leaving you. It was like being rope drunk, but free.

Stretched out next to her and the other two, I passed out, body exerted for the day. I slept, and in my slumber, I awakened several times to find either Veronica or Timothy wrapped around me. The night passed in a blur of dreams and sleepy visions of us all together in the bed.

Morning found us all together still, laying in the giant's bed, curled in strange configurations together. It felt normal, natural to me. Anna woke up next, lifted her head and smiled at me. I smiled and looked at Veronica and her. She lay her head back down on Timothy's chest. Veronica had her arm around my waist and snuggled in closer to her. My arm reached to Timothy's leg, and I put it there.

The day is a strange blur to me now, moments of laughter and genuine surprise as we dressed and went to go find food. As our brunch ends, we segue back to our yards, sitting and talking outside. Dinner was a combo meal of us making the sides, with them making roasted chicken.

It's been several years since we found ourselves together, surprise taking us off and on still. This has felt natural, because it is. Love is love, harm to none. As I lay here between my wife and her lover, Timothy is up making breakfast for us.

Figure Eight

Stepping from the cab, careful not to show too much skin, Rachel slipped out into the chilly night, paying the cabbie with a quick slide of the credit card reader as she closed the door. Turning and facing the desolate looking factory in front of her, she decided that she had the nerves to do this. It'd been something she'd always wanted to do. It had been a few years before she could tell her husband about her wild fantasy of being dominated in a BDSM club, but when she did, his reply shocked her. He wanted her to do it, because it had been one of his too. He wanted to take their bondage and dom/sub relationship public somehow, and thought that this might work for them.

So here she stood in front of the BDSM club, hesitating for a few seconds, steeling her nerves at her fantasy being realized. Quickly she went to the door and slid a second card into the card reader, this one for the club.

The long black hair of her Russian heritage was resting on her shoulders and her face has been excruciatingly made up. She'd taken her time dressing and getting ready tonight. Her excitement had put her on pins and needles all day at work and she shot, and she'd home as soon as possible. She had the next two days off, and had wanted to do this for a few months. Her soft pumps scuffed quietly on the sidewalk as she slid her card into the electronic reader. The metal door responded with a loud thunk as the magnetic lock disengaged.

Rachel walked into the club, unsure if she could find what she was looking for. She wanted to be used, roughly and for as long as the men could go. She was dressed simply, a black leather miniskirt and a tube top of a dark orange vinyl. Her chest was constricted, but that wasn't the cause of her short breaths.

She pulled the door open, and the loud music washed over her. The bass rumbled her chest, and made her nipples stiffen in excitement. Her breathing quickened further as the door clunked shut behind her. The bar and dance floor were full of writhing, dancing people. They were all in various states of undress and to her right, a woman was being fucked by two men on a table.

She stood there watching, joining a small crowd. The woman was watching everyone else, enjoying the attention. After a moment Rachel turned away, looking for the right group of men.

She'd set up a meeting with some guys the week before and was worried they wouldn't show. One of the guys, Alan, slept with her years before, and it'd been a fun night of light bondage. Tonight, she needed more. She'd also rented the new room; it had been updated recently with a new bondage system.

Rachel scanned the table she'd told Alan to meet her at, Alan and the other men. They were all sitting there at the table, smoking and looking out for her. There was a black bag on the table, and seeing it peaked her interest. She slipped over to the table, swishing her hips as she walked.

She stood there, looking them over. Alan looked nerdy, but had beautiful muscles. Billy was tall and thin. The third guy was handsome and seemed to possess a power or aura of command about him. His eyes looked her up and down, and she could see that he was approving of her outfit. Walking up to Alan, she sat on his lap, her mini-skirt slipping up and revealing her shaved groin. As she sat in his lap, the silent Dom had a laser focus on her, eyes burning into her flesh and head like a weapon across a battlefield.

Billy was her husband's ex boyfriend, and Rachel and he had known him for years. In the beginning of the relationship between her and her husband they had several fun nights including Billy. He looked at her with a known longing, and she smiled at him with her eyes on the newcomer.

Alan reached around her to the black cloth bag and unzipped it. He pulled something from it, handing them to her. It was two small vibrators with thick bases to prevent them from slipping too far inside. Standing, she spread her legs and Alan handed her a small tube of lube. Coating the anal vibrator, she bent over, handing it back to Billy. Scraping his chair closer, he took it, inserting it slowly. When it reached its base, she shuddered in delight. Her nipples made impressions in her vinyl top, and the newcomer watched with interest. She glanced back at the newcomer and his eyes were locked onto her groin, and flicked to her eyes. They locked and she felt herself growing warm in her stomach with need.

Standing up, she turned around, looking at the Dom in the eyes as she lubed up the vaginal vibrator. He came next her, his hand wrapping around her wrist. She handed him the vaginal vibrator, and for a moment he stared at it as if he had no idea where it had come from. He pulled the chair out from under the table next to him and sat. Anxious to get started, she sat on his lap facing him.

"Put it in my pussy handsome."

He growled in the dark, eyes burning into hers as she spread her outer labia for him. She sat on the man's knee, the anal vibrator pressed against her flesh, filling her more. A heat had grown in her groin and the twin vibrators fire her up as they start a low hum.

"I'm Thomas" Rachel could already tell he was the dominant one of the group. Actually of the men were, but he was leading the event tonight. He wanted her to know that, and she accepted it willingly.

"Hi Thomas. Ready for a wild night?"

He growled again, low and deep in his throat and she stood looking at the men. The low vibrations of the bullet vibrators were staying consistent, and she placed her hands on the table, leaning forward slightly.

"The safe word is *zaibatsu*. If I say it you will not continue, you will release me from what we are doing."

The men nodded in silence. Thomas was staring at her, his dark eyes boring into her vivid green ones. The men stood. Grabbing the black bag, Alan pulled out a choker made of leather with one large ring on the front and back, and smaller rings spaced evenly around it. He threw it at her and she caught it, turning it over in her hands. Reaching back, she put it on as he pulled one final item from the bag, a chain ornately made up with three leads. Each of the men took one, as Thomas attached the chain to the ring at the back of her collar.

She pulling the keycard from the rental packet for the room, she led the way. She was the submissive, and in a dom/sub relationship even for a night, she had all the power. She felt strange knowing that. The submissive always has the final say, the final word. If they feel unsafe, they always have the safe word to say to stop everything. A good dominant knows how to how to keep their submissive and themselves on the edge of pleasure and pain, just enough pressure to not tip the scales too far left or right.

Rachel walked at an even pace, leading the men through the crowd. As she passed through a hallway crowded with men and women making out in various states of undress and pleasure, someone slapped her ass. She jumped, and then slowed as she felt Alan pull on the chain. The vibrations in her got stronger, and hands groped her ass. She spread her legs apart when someone pushed at her inner thighs, and didn't look back to see who it was. The hands started slipping the vibrators in and out of her, the one in her pussy angled for her g-spot. Her legs trembled as she felt the bullets turned onto the highest setting.

"Don't come," Alan said, his voice strong and clear. She fought not to give into her approaching orgasm, biting her lower lip. She felt the heat rising from her stomach, into her chest, along with a quick flush between her legs. She bit her lip, the pain making the orgasm that was blossoming stop suddenly. She nearly came anyway, even though one of her doms told her not to. Alan turned and stared at her. Just as the orgasm started blossoming again, the vibrations stop. Alan moved closer, and slapped her ass.

"No coming, not yet. If at all."

The foreign pair of hands fell away, and the group continued down the hall. Soon they met a wooden door on their right. This was where they need to go. Rachel reached for the handle and swung the door inwards. The room was lit by several hanging lamps and track lighting rails. In the center of the room was the device she'd been looking forward to for what seemed like ages.

There was an adjustable bed in the center of the room, and this was also a part of her excitement. The center piece was above it, the collection of set pieces that made this scenario so appealing. There was a figure eight of tracks like those used in hospitals to slide privacy curtains back and forth. Throughout the centers of the configuration there were other tracks, which allowed the chains dangling from the ceiling to be positioned anywhere. The adjustable bed was underneath, and small moveable platforms were scattered around the base. The bed itself was like a chiropractor's bed with all of its shifting parts, only on a larger scale.

Rachel shivered in delight, and ran her hands down her length as she stepped into the room. The men followed, letting go of their leashes. Someone gave her a playful push forward, and she stumbled with a giggle. Turning to look, she found Alan pressing down on her shoulder; a silent gesture to signal that he wanted her on her knees. She turned as someone removed the leash.

Alan unzipped his pants, freeing his cock. He shuffled closer, ran the tip across her cheek to leave a trail of pre-come, and then circled her dark purple lipsticked lips. She opened her mouth to wait patiently, as someone behind her pulled off her pumps and slipped leather cuffs onto her ankles.

Alan inserted his cock into her mouth, and she started to suck and swallow him. His cock was musky, like she remembered; it swelled as she deep-throated him. Someone placed a blindfold over her eyes as she sucked, head bobbing, and her hands on Alan's hips. He made grunting noises as the pre-come slicked her tongue, and she slipped her tongue over the head of him as the bobbing continued. Her left hand was squeezed by a cuff, and then her right. Her hands have been taken by Thomas and Billy, raised above her head.

Alan pulled himself from her, his hands on her shoulders for a moment before her vinyl top was slipped off. Hands cupped and fondled her tits, squeezing roughly and pinching at her nipples in that subtle place between pleasure and pain. Her mind was reeling at the sensations of being on that edge of between too much and not enough. She wanted more, but was afraid to speak her needs. Almost as if reading her mind, she felt nipple clamps being placed on her engorged nipples, then a thin chain being placed through the front ring of the choker. She tried to get Alan's cock to her mouth, and the movement pulled on her nipples. The sensation of her nipples being pulled on and the hunger for Alan's cock were a struggle with each other. His hands were in her hair, and she knew his tip was just out of reach without pulling on her nipples. She moved her head back and forth, pulling on the clamps gently to get a feel for the tightness.

Blindfolded, her other senses were heightened. She felt the individual teeth of the clamps surrounding her nipples, the tightness of the choker, and her wet pussy ached with need. Her ass was numb from sitting on her calves, and the air in the room was slightly chilly, making goose bumps rise all over her flesh. Feeling the hair pulled back by the blindfold, her scalp felt strange, a pins and needle like sensation as she bobbed, her nipples pulled on slightly each time that she moved backwards. Her hands were taken behind her and bound. She heard the handcuffs click closed, not leaving her much room to move her arms.

Her mini-skirt was pulled down to her knees, and a paddle thwacked her ass, strong and steady at first.

Alan came, running his hands through her hair and thrusting his hips as he writhed. His thick cock twitched, and she swallowed with enthusiastic grunts of pleasure, as three large spurts of semen slipped down the back of her throat. He pulled back, hands still in her hair. She gasped and rocked at the sudden increase in the force and speed of the paddling, just this side of her threshold. Someone slapped her tits, the clamps jiggling with each slap. Another cock pressed against her open mouth, this one from the side. She licked it, moving to the base and running her tongue to the tip. As she flicked her tongue over the head, the paddling stopped, the numbness was gone, replaced with a warm heat and a sensation like ants crawling on her ass cheeks. As the heat faded, so did the sensation and the cool air made gooseflesh rise again.

Rachel licked the sideways cock, the heat and tingling sensation of arousal moving over her flesh, through her folds, and shooting a triangle of need into her already sensitive breasts. She wanted to come, but it was far too early in the game. She flexed her vaginal muscles tight, shifted her legs underneath her to prevent herself from coming. She felt her juices flowing down her thighs and as it trickled to the floor, it cooled, making her shiver. From her right side, she felt another cock brush her cheek as the two dick heads pressed against each other. Someone from behind grabbed the side of her head, and gently but firmly pulled her to the base of the cock on the left.

She understood the meaning, started licking her way left to right. When her lips and tongue were at the heads, she wrapped her mouth around both of them as best as possible. She flicked her tongue over the tips of both of them, the moans making her hungry for someone to come. Her ass was being squeezed and pinched, and a hand snaked between her legs. It was Alan. She shivered with need as he brushed her pussy with his forearm, started to pinch her inner thighs as she quivered.

She had been licking the tips at the same time as they pressed together, now they moved in front of her. The two of them pressed against her lips, and she took them both in her mouth. Billy started stroking Thomas's cock, and Billy jumped slightly. She felt the rough skin of Thomas's hand brush her lips as he stroked. Rachel heard the men kiss in the darkness around her, heard their subtle moans of pleasure. Thomas's cock was pulled from her mouth, and Billy put more of himself in her, leaving room for the fast strokes of the hand wrapped around him. Suddenly the stroking stopped, and Billy stiffened, coming. One small spurt, and he gasped as he started to pull away from her. She flicked her tongue out to catch the semen, and Billy gasped in pleasure as she smiled secretly.

Thomas put his thicker cock in her mouth, not giving her time to breath, and reaching down, flicked the clamps on her nipples as he thrust into the back of her throat. His hands wrapped around her head, pulled it forward more as his legs started to shake. He came, and she swallowed in fast gulps. The cock in her mouth was bigger than Billy's or Alan's, and she wanted him in her.

Alan stopped pinching her thighs, and she heard a zipper closing as Billy chuckled.

Thomas, spent for the time being, started to go flaccid in her mouth. She growled under her breath as she licked the rest of the come from his tip. Suddenly she was pushed forward onto the carpet; a movement that startled her, made her yip in surprise. Her ass was in the air, and a bare hand slapped her right cheek, hard. The stinging shocked her and she yipped again and again.

"Be quiet."

She bit her lip as a third smack hit her harder than the first two, making her moan. With great care her legs were spread apart, and a warm liquid poured over her ass. The warm lube spread to her pussy and inside her tingling orifices, the movement itself was enough to make her quake. Then the warm lubricant started to work, to leave her sense of touch heightened, the touch of the cool air making her pulse with desire.

Something slipped into her anus, and something else went into her pussy at the same time. With her ass in the air with the mini-skirt around her ankles she felt the soft carpet pull on the nipple clamps, making her wince. It's wasn't too much, but she shifted, repositioned herself just as the thrusts started. Whatever Alan was using it filled her up, his hand on her hips gripping her flesh tightly. The heat grew inside her, traveled quickly upwards to her stomach, and then her chest. Gasping wordlessly, she fought the orgasm. The full sensation of the dildo and cock in her made her moan loudly, as she struggled against the orgasm that bloomed in her. Clenching her hands into fists, she struggled, on the edge of losing her battle. Sweat poured from her face and body, making her skin slick, and Alan lost his grip. He moaned a low, primal sound as he whispered.

"Come! You can come!"

Rachel did, the rush of the double penetration too much to hold back anymore. She felt her fluids slip down her legs and out onto the floor below her, bitting her lip to keep from screaming in pleasure. As the thrusts slowed down, she felt the heat subside and Alan coming loudly again.

The objects slid from her slowly, and she panted into the carpet, her forehead sweating into it. She couldn't stop panting, but now she was being lifted by her arms and the blindfold removed. The men stand there, looked at her like they had a hunger that only she could sate. Alan was removing the strap on, and he tossed it into the dark corner of the room. He was softer than he wanted to be, and the toy had enabled him to pleasure both of them. The other men were naked and hard. Billy had her arms in his hands, and he guided her over to the bed. She felt their caring movements, firm and leading but never cruel; a dom is never truly cruel.

The bed was raised several feet, and the hand cuffs were undone. Her hands swung to her sides, and she raised her arms to get feeling back into them for a moment.

Alan walked over to the thick chains, nodded his head in Thomas's direction, and pushed her back on the bed. Stumbling, she steadied herself on the cool black leather, shivering with anticipation. Billy started to pull levers and push buttons to raise the bed into a different shape. When the bed was done being maneuvered, it became an upside down V with a spot for her knees to rest on.

Thomas took her legs, and one by one bound them; the long chain connected to the ceiling, and her hands cuffed to chains by Billy. The men started to hoist her up, her arms first, then her legs. She faced the bed and the V, confused as to what was going on. She was at least three feet from the bed, and Thomas moved her legs in the chains along the tracks to fold them against her hamstrings, as Billy maneuvered her arms backwards. She let her head lean forward, the handcuffs and chains balanced to where she felt the weight of her body, but not much strain. When the two men were done, she was in a hogtied position. Curious about what was going on, she watched the men surround the bed. They started running their hands over her back, sides, and stomach. The sensation overwhelmed her quickly, her flesh craved it. She was being cared for, the pins and needles worked out of her limbs as they made certain her circulation was restored.

Minutes after the massage started, it suddenly stopped. The warm hands were removed and something was done to the bed. The clicking and popping made her look down; the bed had been put into a level position. She felt her legs being spread by warm hands. Thomas and Alan walked to the front of the bed; Thomas ran his rough fingers over her left cheek in a soft caress.

Alan started to stroke Thomas, his cock in Alan's thick fingers disappearing and reappearing with each stroke. Thomas leaned into Alan, and she jumped as a warm tongue explored her, spread her outer lips and searched for her clit. The lips gently grasped it as the tongue discovered it. The suckling turned her on, but after a few minutes a hungry need made her ache for Thomas again.

As she watched, come spurted from Thomas. The two men continued their touching, and the sight of their passionate making out aroused her as Billy lapped her to orgasm. Billy started to fondle her breasts, pinched the left nipple as his right hand spread her lips apart, slipped a finger inside of her pussy, thrust it in time with the licks and suckling. Rachel glanced downward, looking at Billy's red hair, and then back at Alan and Thomas. Thomas was on his knees, sucking the hard cock as if he'd done this before. The sight of his abandon turned her on even more. He pulled the cock from his mouth, stroked it as he held his mouth open for Alan to come into. The semen splattered on Thomas's chest and cheek instead, but he just rubbed it into his flesh as he stood. He faced her with a gleam in his eyes as he walked over to her. The come on his cheek glistened as he leaned towards her, offered her his cheek.

Her tongue snaked out, licked the stubble of his skin, and collected the semen from him. She swallowed it, and he offered his right nipple where a splotch landed. Taking the nipple in her mouth, she licked and nibbled as Thomas gasped in pleasure. He pulled himself from her and played with her free breast, cupped it and pressed it against her before he let it drop, grinned at the bounce gravity made as it took over.

Billy leaned to the side, and pressed a button, the bed clicking and popping again as it moved to where he could recline on it. While Thomas played with her tits, Billy licked the nipples between Thomas' fingers. The sensation of fingers and tongue on her flesh made her quiver, and Thomas chuckled with satisfaction. He leaned forward, kissed her passionately, and she could taste Alan in his mouth, the effect, intensely erotic. She shivered again, her tits being licked and played with while Thomas started to move her arms.

Her arms were moved in front of her, and the chain was lengthened as she held onto the top of the bed. She was lowered onto Billy, and he slipped himself into her as she shifted to straddle him. The blindfold was put back onto her and her arms were pulled behind her, the chains moving as the darkness surrounded her again. Her legs free, she straddled Billy and rested her body on the platform. The bed clicked and popped, and she felt Billy's breath move from her nipples. He was inside her, and she felt him shudder ready to pound into her, his muscles tight with need.

"Not yet, Billy."

Thomas' voice was a growl that made her tense a little. Alan, who had been silent most of this time, started playing with her ass again, making sure she was open for him. Rachel relaxed, allowing his fingers to explore her. She wanted Thomas' cock in her mouth, if nothing else. She felt Billy and him moving around each other and she went still in anticipation, but when she didn't feel his cock pressing into her open mouth, she furrowed her brow in frustration.

A hand slapped her ass and she tried not to yip, but a small one escaped her. The second slap was on her left cheek, the opposite one. Biting her lip, she kept quiet. Alan had gotten her to open with his fingers, and she gasped as she felt two cocks slip into her ass as one. The sensation of Billy, and the two cocks in her, made her body pour sweat; it ran down her brow and off of her chin. It was almost too much, the pressure almost hurt. She stayed still, kept her body relaxed, and in time the muscles dilated to accommodate them. She knew it was Alan and another toy, but it felt like two men. She took a deep breath, exhaled, and leaned her head forward, hoped for Thomas.

Billy, unable to cope with the sensation that pressed against him through the walls of her pussy and ass, started to thrust, and Alan moved in time with him. She heard flesh on flesh in front of her, and Thomas breathing heavily. She sensed his arousal as the fucking continued, and her body tingled from head to toes. The heat in her grew quicker than before, and the hands that ran over her back and hips pushed her nerve endings over the edge. She rolled her hips, fucking Billy. Her hands behind her, she felt Alan's chest hair barely brush her fingertips, this last sensation tipping her closer to the edge as she moaned louder and longer than she had before.

The double penetration in her ass felt like one thick cock, as her body accepted it deeper inside. In the darkness, she felt the three heads rubbing against each other through the tissue of both walls. Her body enjoyed the full sensation, her nipples as hard as diamonds, as warm fluid sprayed across her left nipple and between her breasts.

Thomas gasped long, ragged breaths, and she knew that he'd come onto her and maybe Billy. Suddenly the thrusting from below stopped, Billy frozen with orgasm. He slipped from her, sprayed on her stomach. A few droplets landed on the underside of her tits, first warm and then cool. The heat grew in her again, and she came all over Billy's groin, the fluid drenching her flesh as much as his. Alan kept pounding for a moment, and then he pulled from her, gasping.

Suddenly her hands were being undone, and she was confused. Thomas took her hands.

"Stand up." Rachel complied, using Thomas' grip to help her onto her quaking legs.

She felt Billy slide from the bed, as she was instructed by Thomas to sit down. Someone helped her swing her legs up onto the bed, and soon she was lying on her back. Her wrists and ankles were rubbed to ensure the circulation was good, and then her feet were rebound, the cuffs tight. The chains were moved, and her legs were brought above her head and to the sides, her ass and pussy exposed. She reached for her knees, but her hands were bound again, brought next to her cheeks with little room to move. She laid her head back from fatigue. Her body started to ache, and she was surprised by how long the men lasted. She was enjoying the attention was receiving tonight.

The mouth on her groin surprised her enough that she jumped and yipped. The mouth slid to her thigh where it bit the tender flesh, hard. She squealed as the bite persisted. The sensation suddenly left and her lips were explored by a tongue that was hungry for her. It found her opening and started to lick, hungry for her taste. She was almost sated, but she still wanted Thomas. As the mouth worked her clit with delicate movements, she felt two different hands on her tits and two dicks pressed against her hands. The chains had been lowered enough to give her room to stroke them, and she started, the slick cocks bobbing as she slipped her hands over them slowly.

The mouth moved from her and for a few precious seconds the ache returned. Rachel knew he must be about to enter her, but wasn't prepared for it when he did. His thick cock filled her, the length and girth inside her making her stop stroking the other men. Billy, or Alan, pinched her nipples, and she started again in time with the thrusts.

Thomas thrust and grunted in pleasure

as she stroked the two other men. She didn't flinch when the come splattered her cheeks, neck, and breasts. She kept stroking them, wanted more semen and orgasms from the men while Thomas fucked her. The man's hands gripped her hips, and he leaned forward to bite her calves. She gasped in pleasure as the bites sent shocks up her legs to her groin which was being thrust against with a sexual fury she'd never felt before. The cock filled her; pressed over and over against her g-spot and the other two spurted again, twitched in her hands as the smaller loads sprayed her gasping mouth with semen.

Her pussy clenched as an orgasm rocked through her, a line of firecrackers from her groin to her mouth. Her eyes clenched tight behind the blindfold, she screamed once, a sound of open almost agonized pleasure.

"Yes!"

Thomas kept thrusting and rolled his hips, hands caressing her flesh and fingers dragging into her skin as he came. He hissed through clenched teeth as the final dregs of his come exploded from him. His thrusts slowly decreased with the fever of need, his hands rested on her stomach, then wrapped around her waist as he leaned forward to kiss her abdomen and climbed up. He kissed her, his hands wrapped around her waist as he buried his head between her breasts.

Rachel felt the other men move away and the chains being lowered, slowly but eventually low enough where they could lie with each other on the bed, the cuffs silently removed. Keeping the blindfold on, she laid there with her husband, running her hands over his back. He gasped, trying to catch his breath to speak, but she shushed him. He slipped the blindfold from her eyes and she stared at him and only him. The other two stepped into the shadows, got dressed and were ready to leave as quietly as possible.

The couple stared at each other, years of love and bonding

making the silence comforting. Several minutes later, they made love, soft and slow, climaxing together. After a rest they slipped from the bed, , moved toward the hidden bathroom, washed in the shower and collected their clothes.

She and Thomas drifted out into the night, left the club hand in hand with her head on his shoulder.

Gagged

Jeffrey woke up, tied to the high-backed chair in his bedroom, nude. He could hear his wife giggling in the hallway, the hardwood floors creaking with her footsteps with what must have been someone else too. He was gagged, a tight cloth wrapped around his mouth, hurting his jaw when he tried to call for help. He looked down at his body, seeing that he was tied with an intricate rope pattern - a pentagram - on his chest, the hemp fibers tight. He could breathe fine, and he recognized his wife's rigging skills instantly. They'd practiced Kinbaku, a rope bondage before, on multiple occasions, but this rigging was different. It seemed to be tighter than normal, and he knew that something new was being introduced tonight. With the Kinbaku, he could allow the stresses of his job literally melt away as the ropes were tied, wrapped, and cinched closed around him.

What the hell? Was I drugged? Who the hell is with her?

The questions bubbled up as he tried his hand restraints, they were tight. His feet were tied to the support bars between the legs, and he knew if he tried to shift his weight around he'd topple the chair. He considered it, but knew it wouldn't do any good. The chair was solidly built and the ropes were tight.

The giggling was punctuated with a squeal from his wife, the one she gave in response to being goosed.

The two of them stepped into the room, unaware he was awake. Zita was half undressed, her full breasts hanging over the dress top, nipples fully erect. It was *that* dress, the special one. It was pulled up over her wide, sexy hips, and her groin was newly shaved. Her friend was a man, and he didn't recognize him, but he was handsome. His square jaw was lined in a five o'clock shadow and his shirt was off. The man wore jeans, no socks. His muscular arms wrapped around his wife from behind, hands squeezing her breasts. They were facing towards the mirror on the dresser across the room, and Zita jumped when she saw him reflected there, watching them.

"Oh! Jeffery! You're awake! This is gonna be fun!"

She walked over to him, running her hand along his smoothly shaved jaw, and then with a quick jolt, slapped him. He jumped, eyes welling with tears from the sharp pain on his cheek. He blinked them away, staring at her. She giggled again and it's that sexy giggle he gets when he's making her feel good. She turned slowly to the man and bent over, her bare ass in his face. Playing with her tits and shaking her ass, she stood and walked towards the man with her hips swaying. Reaching out, she took his belt and undid it, the pants dropping to the floor with a clink of the belt and the rattle of keys in the pocket.

The interloper was standing there still but his eyes were locked on his wife. He was a bit taller than Jeffery, and all muscles from his shoulders to his hips. The blonde hair stood out from his tanned form. Jeffery was in decent shape, but this guy was hot. He could see why Zita would want him, his wife too. Jeffrey was always wondering why she married him, outside of the deep love they had for each other. He wasn't ugly but he wasn't much to look at. Looking the man in the eyes, he saw a hunger there. He couldn't place it, but the hunger reminded him of his college years, when he saw someone that turned him on and he wanted them. The man turned to Zita, his back to Jeffery. Jeffery's heart started pounding, and his headache from earlier returned stronger than ever.

What the fuck? Oh… Oh god.

Her long red hair was in a honeycomb, and as she pulled down the man's boxers, she looked over her shoulder at him. The large cock bounced free, hard and ready for her, and she started stroking it while staring her husband in the eye. Zita's other hand started tracing lines on the interloper's chest, pinching the nipple on the right, slowly tracing a pattern to his balls. She turned towards him and they kiss. A passion filled kiss that enraged him, but also turned him on. He sat there, unable to stop his wife as she explored the man in front of him. The tears were gone, but his eyes as he blinked them a few times.

The man slid the dress off of her, nipping at her tits and nipples as it swooshed past her hips and gathered at her feet. She kicked the silk dress that he bought her for sexy occasions under the bed. As Zita let her lover explore her with his hands, she kept stroking his long, thick cock. Jeffery can't help but stare at it, wondering if it feels better than his. Wondering if that's the reason why she's doing this.

He had a momentary memory surface, but it dipped back into his whirling mind as the cock started spurting come on his wife. It splattered her lower stomach, thick and clinging where it landed. She let go of his balls and started rubbing it into her skin. He felt wracked with frustration. He was getting hard, but he was also jealous. His wife never let him come on her, even on accident. She told him she found it gross, not demeaning, but unappealing. She turns to look at him again.

"This is a big cock. I like it a lot. I could beat him off for hours."

I'm not small, god damn it. I'm thicker than he is.

He looks down, and his cock is erect too, pre-come is flowing from the tip. It's thicker than the other man's, he smiles as much as he can behind the gag. His eyes are boring into his wife's back, as he watches the thick fingers of the lover spread her ass cheeks apart.

Zita's kissing and biting his shoulder, she doesn't flinch as he spreads her ass further. Slipping his middle finger over and then into her asshole, he starts playing with it as his left hand snakes to her hair. He pulls the sticks holding it up and it tumbles down, covering her back and the top of her ass. She's leaning against him as thick fingers start to play with her pussy and her hips start to thrust back into his left hand. Tipping her head back, she moans. She's coming onto her lover's hand and he's licking it, staring at him. Their eyes lock and there is a mutual lust in his eyes. He stops playing with her ass, pushing down on her shoulders. She drops to her knees, still kneading and stroking the hardon in her right hand. She has him twist to the left so her husband can watch her suck him off. She reaches her hot tongue out, flicking it across the head a few times before she takes the head in her mouth and starts bobbing. Stroking his cock, Zita takes more of it into her mouth, stroking less with each inch she takes in.

She can suck, that's for sure. He won't last long. I can, damn it.

Jeffrey watches as the cock makes her cheeks puff in and out with each stroke of her throat. He sees the dickhead making her throat push out as she bobs, and it grosses him out. She takes a few less inches and keeps a steady rhythm for a long time. The man stiffens, hands wrapping around her face as he gets her to stop bobbing. She does and he watches as she swallows four or five times. Slipping the semi soft cock out of her mouth she rubs the tip over her lips, her left cheek, staring at him with her head turned.

"God, he tastes as good as he smells."

She walks over to where Jeffrey's tied and kisses his forehead. He wants to head butt her, but doesn't.

"It'll be fine, tiger! You've got a hard-on so you must be enjoying something!"

Her breath smells of the come she's swallowed, it smells musky and it arouses him, makes his cock a bit harder, he blinks a few times. She turns around and bends over spreading her outer lips. Jeffrey's staring at her pussy as she plays with herself, suspended over his cock. He thinks she's going to squirt onto him, her moans getting close to the point of orgasm as she fingers herself for him. The man has climbed onto his bed, *their* bed, and pulls a small tube from her drawer. He flicks it onto the bed and he snaps back to looking at his wife. She's scooted herself a bit forward, and she squirts her orgasm on the floor in front of the chair, using the edge of the bed for balance.

Mmm… that smell.

The smell of his wife fills the room and his nostrils flare at it. He knows it well, having been drenched in it for years. It makes him ache for her, to touch her, make her come for him. This moment freezes for a few seconds and Zita's climbing onto the bed. The lover slips off, allowing her to lie in the center of it. She spreads her legs, and the lover climbs over her left leg to grab the tube. He can't see what's going on, but the moans as his head is buried between his wife's legs tell him.

The right arm of the lover is bobbing back and forth and her hands are in his short blonde hair, head tilted back. The lover's legs are spread, his ass is in the air, and he's looking at it. It's relatively bare and his cheeks are sexy as they bounce. He's watching the cock bob and brush against the comforter as he licks and fingers his wife. Then he notices his wife in the midst of this. Zita's eyes are open, staring him dead on. Her mouth makes little O's of pleasure, but her eyes never leave his. Legs snapping shut around the lovers head, she freezes and her eyes slip shut. Her body twitches several times with a powerful orgasm, and then slowly her legs relax. The guy slips next to her, left hand pinching and bouncing her right tit as he sucks and bites the left.

Wow. She's hot. I knew she was, but god damn she's hot. I'd kill to fuck her right now.

The two are staring at him, six eyes locked together. He knows what's going to happen next when she brushes the guy away and crawls to the edge of bed. Her ass is in the air and her left hand snakes between her legs.

She looks back at the blonde- haired man.

"Fuck me, *hard*, please?"

The two stare at him and his bobbing cock. It's coated in pre-come, from tip to base on the side facing them.

"See, he wants you to fuck me. Right baby?"

The thoughts and emotions rolling through him make it difficult to breathe. Jeffrey's staring at them, eyes unblinking. He knows what he wants, needs. He fights the emotions rolling through him, but he loses.

He nods, once.

The bonde-haired man, looking at his wife as she wiggles her ass, smiles. He scoots closer and enters her. As the man slips inside inch by inch, the ropes across his chest feel tighter. Jeffrey's cock needs attention, *he* needs attention. He craves hands, a mouth or an ass on his cock. He wants to come, but can't. He wants to do many things to his wife, but he's tied here.

The two start fucking hard and fast, moaning loudly with their eyes screwed shut in pleasure. She's reaching back and fingering herself as she's fucked. Their bodies are bouncing and writhing in time with each other. The hands on her shoulders go to her hips, then her ass cheeks, and he knows with the little jump there is a finger or thumb in her ass as the cock pounds inside her.

Wow. Oh god, wow. They're beautiful together. I must admit that.

Suddenly, the hands pull her back and the bodies shift. She's riding him, his hands exploring her pussy and clit as she's staring at her husband. Their eyes lock and freeze for seconds. Her hands go to her tits, squeezing and bouncing and the interloper bites her neck, her shoulder. She leans against him, and moans loudly as she squirts fluid across his body. The man's cock is coated in her juices, and he sees him pull out, head coated in come. It squirts a few seconds as he pulls out, coating her outer lips and her ass with come as she climbs to the edge of the bed. They slip off of it, and move to the chair. The man is on his right, she's on his left. She leans close, and whispers.

"Wow. Want to taste him? Want to taste me and him?"

The man moves closer, and speaks in a quiet tone.

"Don't scream. Don't yell. Or else."

He reaches back, cock still hard the two of them brushing tips ever so softly as the gag is loosened, and he slips it down. Rebecca takes the hard cocks, and rubs them together. The lover hushes him, as the moan starts to escape his lips. She lets the cocks go and they look at each other.

Jeffrey's far back on the chair, and the man stands right in front as Zita undoes the center rope tying him to the chair and he leans forward slowly, hands still tied. The cock is bobbing in front of him, and his mouth opens slightly at the scents coming from it. He's aroused and knows what he wants to do. His wife starts stroking his cock and he takes the offered one into his mouth. The scents and tastes of his wife and her lover are intermingled. The bitter taste of semen with the overpowering scent of his wife's juices turn him on. Her left hand is stroking the cock in his mouth, but it slides away over time. He tastes them both and he wants them.

She'd never let me fuck him. Right?

He bobs into Jeffrey's mouth as he's spurting come all over her hands and the man's thighs. The blonde-haired man is moaning in pleasure as he comes too. The blonde-haired man's hands are gripping his face, his hair and he keeps bobbing, pleasuring him into a second oral orgasm. He swallows the thick come, the scent of musk overpowering the taste of his wife.

As the orgasms in the men fade, everyone slowly backs

away, breathing heavily and looking at each other.

The married couple stares at each other even longer. He speaks words he never thought he'd ask.

"Can I fuck him? Please?"

She stares at him, and shakes her head.

"No. He can fuck you."

The man nods once at her, staring at him for a reply. Still tied there he doesn't know what to expect, but gasps in pleasure when the answer is revealed. She picks a condom pack up, and slips it on him. The second part is trickier. When the condom is on, the blonde-haired man stands in front of the chair, hands between his legs. With the grace of a gymnast, he raises Jeffrey's legs from the sides and wraps them around him and the back of the chair. While still balancing himself, he starts to sink the cock into his ass, one achingly slow inch at a time. The man starts slowly sinking himself on him, hands balancing his body at just the right angle, perfectly still. The weight of the man on his lap isn't too unbearable, especially with the pleasures of the tightening and loosening ass wrapped around him. The thrusts start short and fast, and then lengthen as he gets the right rhythm down.

This! Ohmygodthis! Fuck me!

The two men are staring at each other and the husband starts biting the chest and nipples of his lover. He jumps when his wife's hand clasps around the now hard cock and starts stroking it, between the men. He comes quickly, filling the condom, and the blonde-haired man comes on his chest, his stomach as his wife's strokes. She's kissing them both, free hand touching and squeezing soft and hard parts on her men.

The three slowly disengage from each other. Her hands leave them, and he stops nibbling and biting the lover. The lover lifts himself, still graceful as she starts unbinding her husband. The rope cuffs loosen first, and he allows his muscles to relax as the rigging is undone, he doesn't move, at first watching intently. The lover has grabbed his pants and is slipping out of the door to the hallway. He looks at her, motioning for a kiss. As the final ropes are loosened and the blood flows back to Jeffrey's body they kiss deeper.

"Well done, dear. That was perfect."

Zita smiles and presses her forehead against his, kissing him soft and gentle.

"Good. Good."

Inside Out

Isaac pulled up to the crappy gravel parking lot of the dive bar he used to love. It was getting dark, but there were a few vehicles in the parking lot. There was a school bus, a beat to hell Jaguar, two equally crappy pickup trucks and two motorcycles in the lot. It wasn't popular anymore, but the bar was still kind of busy on Friday and Saturday nights. On a Thursday, it was practically dead. The long, flat-topped building was made of wood, and with his window down he should have been hearing the jukebox pumping through the crappy speakers throughout the building. Clicking the window up, he climbed out of his much nicer car. He popped the locks and waited for the double beep. He didn't expect any problems, especially on a quiet night like this, but he was a little worried. Issac stood there, feeling unsure if he'd even find what he was looking for. He wanted sex, just sex, from someone tonight. Male, or female he wanted to fuck.

It'd been too long, and there'd been too many missed chances in his day to day life to make a relationship with someone. It's why he came to dives like this, finding the momentary release of orgasm helped him think he'd be ok for awhile.

Crunching along the side of the building, he heard music faintly through the thin walls. The gravel was a sea of TV static in the growing dark, and a few rocks were kicked forward by his feet as he walked. Running his hand along the windowless wall, he felt the heat from the sun beating down on it for the last twelve hours. This side of the building faced west, and in the desert sun it got unbearably hot during the day. At the wooden double doors he took a deep breath and turned the knob; stepping into the small foyer, he pushed the interior glass door open.

There were about ten people in the place. The two motor-cyclists, a few seats down from them a large burly man with overalls on, and sitting to his left in a booth a middle-aged woman who looked like she'd seen some shit in her life. Two thin guys in beat to hell clothes were playing pool, and another woman was sitting on the far side of the bar, next to the wall. He walked up to the bar, his feet making the floor bong and creak with every step. Suddenly he felt like he stood out in his casual business clothes. His button-up shirt and khaki's were offset by a pair of scuffed loafers that he had worn for the last year. No one paid him any attention, not even the bartender.

He cleared his throat and the bartender looked over with a look a lizard would give prey on a day too hot to move.

"Vodka on the rocks, three fingers."

"Fifteen fifty." The bartender bent down, grabbed a bottle and started pouring.

He pulled a twenty, slid it across the slick bar and took his drink. To the far left of the bar were the restrooms and some more booths in the dark. Feeling out of place in his attire, he stood and looked at the back of building. He took the darkest booth he could find and pulled the ashtray closer to him. Lighting up, he inhaled, exhaling into the drink before him. He lifted it and took a sip, the alcohol burning his nostrils and throat as it went down. It was good vodka and he smiled to himself. Taking another sip, he smoked in silence. He wasn't sure if he would find what he was looking for, especially tonight. He needed someone to take home, to fuck them silly and send them on his or her way. No one here was good looking enough, and there wouldn't be any bisexual or gay men here tonight. With a larger group of people, maybe. The burly man certainly wasn't his type, and the women didn't do anything for him either, so he decided to wait an hour and see if things picked up.

A quick glance at his watch told him that it was only nine thirty, or a hair before. He pulled his phone from his pocket, checked his social media sites and found nothing hopping. Yeah, he knew he should just get an app or something for random meet-ups, but he missed the days of organically finding someone.

Ten minutes later he exhausted half the cash on him, and had another vodka in front of him. The bartender wouldn't appreciate the tips, but he gave them anyway. He was into his third smoke when the outer doors opened, and he saw a woman step into the foyer through the glass push doors inside.

She was tall, with long, curly red hair to her waist. Part of it was the six or seven inch heels on her fuck-pumps, but he could tell she was naturally tall. She was wearing a black, almost see-through dress, and from the overhead light he knew that she wasn't wearing any underwear. Her pale flesh shone through the sheer material, and her dark nipples seemed to contrast with her skin. She walked in, pushing the door open and scampering through. She stood at the doorway for a few seconds, scanning the patrons, and then walked to the bar, her heels not affecting her balance on the uneven wooden floor. He couldn't hear what she ordered, but the bartender shook his head and pushed back the bill she slid across the bar to him before he made her drink.

Staring at her from behind, he could see the mounds of her ass, as large and pale as the rest of her. The dress was tight, but she seemed to flow like water as she turned with her orange drink and started walking to the booth in front of his. Isaac looked down at his phone, ignoring her now. He didn't want to seem like the rest of the men in the bar, and the women too. The bar had grown silent, as quiet as such a place could be, and they all stared at her as she walked. The tension in the bar was high all of a sudden. Every man in the place wanted her, and the women wanted to be her.

He jumped when she sat down across from him. He dropped his phone and looked up quickly in shock.

"Can I sit here? They're all acting like they want to jump me. I shouldn't have come." She had a whiskey and cigarette voice that he found instantly hot, and she was whispering. Her voice reminded him of Gillian Anderson, someone he found beautiful.

He nodded slightly and she relaxed as she sipped her drink. Coughing a little, she stopped to stare into it. He sat there, looking her in the eyes, the lamp over the table showing her breasts perfectly through the dress. Her nipples were hard as she started staring back at him.

"I'm Isaac, and I shouldn't have come here either."

She giggled at this, a strange sound in the bar that started resuming its activity. He stared down at his phone, the blank screen reflecting him. Glancing up, he noticed that her drink was half gone already.

"Holy crap! You want another one?"

"No, I want to finish this and get out of here. This was a bad night to come."

He nods, slips his phone into his pocket and his pack of smokes go in the other.

He starts to stand and she whimpers quietly. He plops his ass down softly, the vinyl seat making a farting sound. She giggles again and drains the rest of her drink.

"What made you come here? Tonight, I mean."

Isaac looked at his half-full drink and decides to tell the truth, knowing that this woman would never sleep with him.

"Uh, I came here to find someone to fuck."

She nodded, unperturbed, and pulled a smoke from her

purse. He offered her his lighter. She lit it and blew smoke into the light above them, the light shade collecting it. He sits there as she stares at him. He feels her look over his balding head, his stomach that sticks out a bit and his chest. Her head tilted back some, her violet eyes searching his for something. Sitting there for several more minutes as she smokes, he sees her nod once, then twice. Stubbing her smoke out, she stands, and nods her head towards the door. Mike isn't sure what the hell is going on, but he follows her lead.

In the foyer, as he held the door open for her, she whispered to him.

"Follow my car."

They walked out into the chilly night, and Mike saw her visibly shiver. She pointed at a nice Audi and he walked to his car. She climbed into hers, and they seemed to fire the engines in their cars at the same time. She backed out, and he followed. He had a Chrysler LHS, it was a deep maroon red. He wanted to pace it against the Audi, but he followed her instead. Keeping the radio off, he followed her in silence, amazed that such a woman would want him. He wanted her. He felt his cock grow along his left thigh, the heat almost too much to bear. They travelled the back roads, going from the paved blacktop to a dirt road, and he got worried this was a scam. He'd heard about guys being lured to a private location and then robbed. Sometimes they were just beaten, other times they were killed. He didn't want to be hurt, or robbed, but he traveled on.

Finally her right blinker came on at the end of a long drive way. The house was set far back from the road, and a gate was built into the fence. The gate slid open and she pulled in, Isaac followed after her. It slid closed behind him, and he jumped a little. It probably had a motion detector for when he wanted to leave, but he got worried again. They pulled up to the half circle drive and she turned off her engine. He turned his off and climbed out. She was waiting for him at the doors. The doors were large and he thought that she might need help opening them. Surprising him, she swung the right one open like it was made of feathers and they stepped into the large foyer. He was shocked that she had a place like this, but he didn't care after a few seconds.

His need drove him to her; walking almost too quickly he was next to her in a moment. She must have wanted him badly too, because she reached out for him when he was still a few feet away. They embraced, kissing passionately. Isaac's hands wandered to her ass cheeks, squeezing them tightly. She responded by pressing her body closer to his and unbuttoning his shirt. It fell to the floor; her hands were running over his chest and across his muscular shoulders. Her hands slid down his back, making him shiver in delight. His nipples were hard as rocks and as she started squeezing his ass, she bent down to lick them.

Sliding his hands against the extremely smooth cloth and upwards, his hands end up on her shoulders. The dress had thin straps that kept the dress on her. He slid them down and pulled the dress to her waist. Her breasts swelled in arousal as he watched and he cupped them, leaning back from her to get her to stop licking him. She responded by pulling away and pressing her breasts together with her arms. He started at the tops of her breasts, licking and biting gently, first the left, then the right. Trailing his tongue down the left one, he took her nipple in his mouth. Flicking his tongue over the half inch long nipple, his pants are undone and fall to the floor. He pulled a few inches from her and kicks off his shoes, stepped out of his pants. While he stepped out of them, she pulled off the dress. Her thong the only thing keeping her from being nude; she walked over to the staircase, glancing over her shoulders at him. When she reached the staircase she looked back at him, and lifted her right leg, and arched it back. She slipped the heel under the thin material between her ass cheeks, with a kick they're pulled down to her ankles and another kick sends them flying to the left.

Isaac stared, turned on that she could do that, and he

started after her up the stairs. She ran up the stairs, her balance perfect as she led him. They reach a bedroom; the door is wide open to show a warmly lit room with a four post bed in the center. She stalked over to the bed, turned around and sat on the edge. She beckoned him with her right hand as she started fingering herself with her left. He walked in, and to her. She pulled his boxers down with her free hand, then gripped his ass cheek to pull him closer. He slipped out of the boxers, his cock bobbing as he stepped closer. Her beautiful breasts rose and fell slowly with each breath. He stared at them; her left hand snaked behind him, to his ass. He spread his legs a little and her middle finger slipped inside him as he scooted closer. With her right hand she stroked him, and his hands went to her shoulders while he leaned back. Eyes closed, he felt his orgasm building and he snapped them open, staring into her eyes as he came between her breasts. She gave him a wicked smile, and he came again from the stimulation in his ass her fingers brought him.

With two splotches of come on her chest, she rolled over onto her hands and knees and spread her legs. Isaac was still hard, and he wanted inside of her. Moving closer, he spreads her legs a little more, and gripping his hot member in his left hand he slides inside her. She pressed against him, thrusting back in time with him. His hands on her hips, he moaned loudly as he closed his eyes. A few seconds later, she's moaning too, louder than him as he felt her pussy tighten around him.

"On top, I want you on top!"

Isaac slid from her, moving to the edge of the bed.She flipped over onto her back, reaching for him. He slipped onto the bed, then inside her with her legs thrown over his shoulders. Her hands snaked to his ass, nails digging in as he came inside her. Pumping harder as he came again, she gasped as a third orgasm rolled through her.

Isaac slipped from her, lying on his stomach, breathing in and out. She threw her right leg over him, running her hand over his back.

"Can I show you something?" She whispered in his ear, and he nodded, ready to fall asleep. He struggled to pull his eyes open as she got him to lie on his back.

She straddled him, spreading her labia open, and her eyes closed tight. Suddenly something shifts in her groin and he freaked a little. A penis head emerges from her vulva, as he stared in horror and an involuntary excitement. The penis is thick, about three inches, and it comes out to almost eight inches in length. Her eyes opened, and they locked like laser beams on his. Her eyes were pleading, looking at her groin and then his eyes, rapid movements that betrayed the strong exterior.

Holy crap! She's got a cock!

He looks at her, unsure of how to respond. So he does the simplest thing.

"Is this your... secret?"

Her eyes burning into him, demanding an answer, she nods.

"Do you want me still? Do you want me?"

Seconds felt like hours, and Isaac knew that this was something he'd dreamed of for years, finding a *futanari*, a woman with a hidden penis. It was something he'd discovered in anime, a trope but he found the idea hot, having the penis and vagina in a woman. He was bisexual and this turned him on. Now he was staring at a real life *futanari*.

He nodded letting her know that he still wanted her. She moved forward, and his mouth opened for her penis. Taking it in as deep as he can, he starts bobbing, tasting her fluids mingled with his. It drives his lust for her, and he takes her as deep as the position allows. He pulled her from his mouth, and pressed against her stomach. She slid off and laid on her back, legs spread far apart. He moved between them, licking the length of her and sucking on the tip. Her hands were in his hair and she gasped in pleasure, the sensations making her shiver in pleasure.

He deep throated her, squeezing her tip with the back of his throat as he bobbed and licked with what little room he had. She stiffened, and soon he swallowed her come. His cock was hard again, but he wanted her in *him.* He pulled away from her, her cock was still hard. He climbed on the bed, raising his ass in the air. She crawled on the bed behind him, leaned down, licked his ass and slipped her fingers in him.

He opened quickly, desire pushing him to take her. She moved to a bed stand and pulled something from it. He whimpered, thinking it would be a condom, but it was lubricant. She applied it to him, he gasped in pleasure as the tip pressed against his ass. He steadied himself and he turned his head to moan in pleasure as she started sliding into him. It's the largest cock he'd taken and it filled him. The pressure was tight, and he willed himself to relax a little more. She was deep in him when her hands went to his back, then his shoulders.

She started thrusting hard and fast, stroking his hard cock with her left hand as she gripped his shoulder with her other hand. Her hands went back to his shoulders and she thrusted harder, pulled on him. Taking her left hand from his shoulder, she tried to get him hard again, but he was spent, but the pressure in him felt too good to stop. The thrusts slowed as she came, and he felt the orgasms pump into him. He gasped in time with her last orgasm, and she slid from him, deflating as she pulled out. As she laid next to him, her flaccid penis retracted into her body.

He turned over to her, pulled her into his arms and sleep pulled him down. They spent the night curled together, a tangle of arms and legs wrapped up in each other. When he awoke in the morning, she'd left a note.

Isaac,

Thank you for last night. It's been years since I've been able to be myself with someone. I want to know if you want to spend more time with me.

Lucinda

He found her phone number at the bottom of the sheet, and entered it into his phone. He doesn't know if she gave him her real number, but he decided to call it later. Gathering his washed clothes a he headed to the door, amazed at the beauty of her house. His footsteps echoed in the empty halls and rooms, but it wasn't a lonely trek. The house was full of curiosities and trinkets from everywhere, small coins from India, a skull from some strange animal in Africa. He walked and examined everything, a small museums worth of items. As he reached the large wooden doors, he turned and looked again at the house. Nervous that she might have lied to him about her number and too scared to try it now, he left in silence.

Standing on the patio, he lit a smoke and watched his exhalations float into the morning sky. More secure in his choice to call her later. He walked to his car, found his keys and drove home uncertain what she was but aware he wanted more.

LEATHER HANDCUFFS

I had arrived at the club a few hours earlier, needing some sort of release, sifting lifelessly through the people here. I was sitting on a leather couch in the main room, watching a woman spank a man with various paddles. He was bent over her knee and yelling each time he was whacked. Finally she found the right type of paddle, a velvet covered wooden one, and his yells turned into whimpers.

I lost interest in them, enjoying his pain from a distance, when an other walked in. He was shorter than her, but muscular. She was tall and a little lighter than he was, her long black hair flowing down to her lower back. His face was a rock carved out of a life of pain and misery, but he looked happy enough in this moment. They saw me sitting on the couch, legs spread apart, my cotton pants hiding my shrinking hard-on from watching the paddling. Both of their eyes locked onto mine, as they moved through the fairly crowded room to the couch I was sitting on. I sat up, taking a sip of my vodka.

He sat on my left, she on his. He leaned close to my ear and whispered "Men or women? Sub?"

"Both. Bi submissive."

"Good, we can both play. We have a room rented already. Come?"

I sat there, thinking. They were cute, but a strange couple. It'd been awhile since I had a couple want me. I wanted to jump up and run to the room, but I sat there. I looked at my drink, and then glanced sideways at him. I leaned a bit further to look at her. She looked at me back, nodding.

So, they're here to have fun too. Fuck it, let's do this.

I nod once, and they stand first. She walks over to me, and clipped a leash to my collar. I wear it all the time, even though I have no dom or domme. To signify that I was taken I'd have a small padlock on the front ring but I didn't have one, so they saw were in luck. The leash tugged on me, and I followed them through the crowd; making sure there was just enough slack that it wouldn't get tangled up.

At the door, he turned to me.

"Safe word?"

"Zaibatsu."

They entered the room, and the demeanor changed to something that I needed. The room was simple, a bed in the center with a standing closet and several dressers. In the center of the open space was an exposed rafter with chains hanging down. I felt my skin go electric at the sight of it. Being lead directly under the chain I felt my heart pound in my ears. I was eager to be tied and used, had craved it for a long while.

The urge to be bound made the room swim, and I stood still in the room. The couple put their loose items on an easy chair and they turned to focus on me.

"Undress. Stand right there when done."

I did so, collar unclipped in swift and efficient manner. My shirt came off first, then my pants. I stood in my boxers, afraid of showing my growing erection. I didn't want to offend them by seeming too eager but I needed this. I pulled off my boxers and put them on top of my pants. I stood there, hands behind my back, waiting. He curled his fingers to stand closer to the chain as the room spun in anticipation. He stalked over to me, having pulled an eye mask from a drawer, and I bent my head forward for it to be tied.

Now I was being tied up to the rafter with leather hand-cuffs, m hard-on bobbing as the chain attaching me to the rafter was locked into place, the vibrations echoing through my body. My eye mask was tight, but since it was made of felt or something similar, it didn't dig into my skin. I felt my legs get spread apart, and my nipples were hard enough that I could feel them hardening in arousal. My cock was harder than normal, and my lungs were working overtime with how fast I was breathing. I love light bondage, but this was different, more primal than I'd ever experienced. Through the thick walls, I heard the bass of the crappy techno playing in the club next door. My heart was going a mile a minute because I didn't know what to expect, and yet I knew wanted it.

I felt was a cock ring being slipped over my tip, and down the shaft. At the base, I felt a clicking as the ring tightened around my cock. I jumped a little as someone slapped my ass. Jumping in response, I got slapped again, firmer this time. Something a little too tight was clamped down on my nipples quickly, and I did my best not to jump. I couldn't help it, but this time the expected slap didn't occur. I felt my legs being pushed further apart, almost uncomfortably, but I held onto the leather handcuffs. They surrounded my wrists, and my fingers wrapped firmly around the chain.

I felt a mouth slip onto my bobbing member, hot and wet. My lover took me as deep as they could, and slowly slid back. The lips were indistinguishable, but the sounds of pleasure as I was bobbed languorously on were male. I felt something thick pressing against my asshole, and a hand was suddenly on my chest, pushing me back slightly. I felt the tip of the object slip into me, then another half inch. It stayed there, hanging out of me while a hand started exploring my chest. The hand slipped to my left nipple as the object slowly started to thrust. I gasped slightly at the sensation, my ass and cock being pleasured at the same time. The left nipple hurt a little, but I tried to ignore it. I felt my balls descend, dropping a good three inches, and knew I was about to come. I stiffened slightly, and the bobbing quickened. I came, three large bursts, and he swallowed each one. The mouth pulled away from me, and I sensed him moving behind me.

I frowned, unsure of what was going on, but suddenly fingernails were running down my back. I hissed between clinched teeth, the pain hurting. The claws reached my ass cheeks as the thrusting started again, going deeper into me. The claws clenched my ass cheeks, one of my favorite turn-ons. As the fingernails were removed, I felt the dildo go even deeper; my ass opening. Finally it sunk to the base. I felt full, and I relaxed a bit more to make it feel better. The pressure inside me was almost too much, it was slightly bigger than what I had before.

The pressure on my arms dangling left, and I stepped back as my hands came free; legs wobbly from the stance I had been in. I managed to dodge smacking myself in the head with my own exhausted arms, but the leather handcuffs remained. I felt hands pushing down on my shoulders. I obeyed and got on my knees, legs still spread apart. The dildo felt good in my ass, but I wanted more. Suddenly, a cock was brushing my lips, and I licked the tip. Opening my mouth, he put himself as far back as I could take. He tasted of flesh, and a spice I couldn't quite make out, something exotic that filled my nostrils. Breathing in his scent and her scent that came to me suddenly, I started bobbing.

My lips wrapped around the edges of my teeth, as I started going down his shaft, gripping him firmly. I was salivating a little; it lubed my lips and him as I started bobbing a little deeper each time. I felt my throat open up slightly, and took him in more. When his tip was near the back of my throat, I made a swallowing motion and started bobbing slowly as I continued to massage his tip with the back of my mouth. His hands went to my head, and I started doing the squeezing a bit more. He stopped thrusting his cock forward when he came, and I swallowed in two quick gulps. His semen tasted bitter, with an edge of the strange spice that I'd smelled in him. It was almost Indian, a curry-like spice, and I wanted more.

I started bobbing again, taking less into my mouth over the next few seconds, until just his tip was in my mouth. I started flicking my tongue over his slit, and going in a circular motion afterwards for a few seconds. He came again, and I savored the taste of his come. Swallowing it after I pulled away from him, I risked a smile. A soft hand caressed my jaw line, and my right nipple was twisted a little. I hissed in pain, and I felt the clamps being removed. My nipples felt strangely naked, and it bothered me. What bothered me more was that I could feel my pulse in them. The thrum made them hurt more now that the clamps were off than it when they were on. I sensed the man moving behind me, and he started pushing against the base of the dildo. I slumped forward with my ass in the air.

The dildo was extracted slowly and when it was out, I felt an instant ache of need. The warm lubricant was spread on my asshole, and a little inside. The cock I had just sucked was suddenly in me, deep and thick. In my mouth, the tip had been the size of a good strawberry; now that cock was deep inside me. His thighs were pressing against mine, and the heat of his flesh in and against me felt phenomenal.

Before I knew it he was fucking me hard and fast, my ass cheeks bouncing in rhythm to his thrusts. I was moaning in pleasure, and the warm hand that wasn't his enveloped my cock, stroking. I was aroused and came quickly, the cock ring doing its job of keeping me hard. It wasn't painful yet, but much longer and I'd hurt tomorrow morning. Suddenly the thrusting stopped, and I felt the pulse of the semen through his cock; three squirts and he pulled free.

I lay there, lost in a fever of arousal and exhaustion. I was panting and coated with sweat, still wanting to fuck or be fucked all over again. My arms were stretched out before me, and I felt the leather handcuffs being removed. I twisted and turned my wrists in all kinds of directions to get the cramps out. I got on all fours, slowly and then onto my knees. My cock was rock hard still, and I wanted to be in someone. I felt her move close to me, her breasts brushing my chest. I reached out, hands finding her shoulders after a few misses, and I ran my hands down her chest. I reached for her breasts and squeezed them, finding the nipples short but rock hard. I pinched and pulled, provoking a gasp of delight from her. Still playing with her right breast, my hand snaked to her groin as I explored her outer folds. My finger slipping inside her, she leaned forward, kissing me suddenly. I felt hands start to run up and down my back and ass, spreading my ass cheeks. She came, tightening around my finger; short gasps escaping her lips as we parted.

She pulled herself from me, and I felt the hands leave my ass. The man moved in front of me, my bobbing hands finding his ass cheeks. I spread them and let them bounce. I held my hand out, and a condom was handed to me. I bit the wrapper open on the corner and pulled it free, wrapping my cock in it. His ass was open and ready when I slipped into him, hands on his shoulders. I started rolling my hips fast and hard, him pressing back against me, moaning loudly. I felt my breath hissing out of me, eyes clenched shut behind the mask, as I fucked him hard. I came, four bursts of semen filling the condom. I kept going, thrusting and pulling on his shoulders at the same time, for several minutes. Finally he came himself, slumping over, then down onto the soft carpet. The condom slipped off as he moved to the floor, and I was free. Reaching up to take off the mask, I kept my eyes closed.

I slowly opened them to the dimly lit room, and the sight of my lovers lying side by side, ready to pass out. I stood, legs barely holding me, and went to the toilet in the corner. I sat, undoing the cock ring slowly. I pissed, slowly at first, then a stream that hurt. I was a little worried, but by the time I was done it didn't hurt so much. Walking over to the clothes rack, I picked up my stuff and got dressed. As I left I locked the door behind me, and gave a little wave to the sleeping couple.

They've not come back again since, even though I keep dreaming of them, of her. I keep envisioning the things that I'd want to do to her while her man watched. I'd let him join in maybe, but I kept thinking of her. The smell of her on my hand lasted for hours after I showered. I can't get her long black hair out of my mind. So I return consistently to the club, hoping for them to come back, all to no avail. Here I sit watching a man lead a woman on a chain through the main foyer, unexcited by the figures playing and hurting each other all around me.

I want to play with people and couples, but it is her, them as a couple I want to have return. To be sitting on my couch, the one the bouncers leave empty for me because I am here almost every night. The club moves around me, lives passing by me that I could be interacting with, but not the life or lives that I want. So, here I sit and drink. Waiting and craving the leather hand cuffs.

LOVERS

He didn't know what he wanted, but he knew he needed *something*. He sat in front of his computer looking through his tabs. They were all about gaming, the paranormal, the news, and in the last tab, a new chat service his internet company had come up with. He was browsing in the darker side of the user created rooms. There were fantasy rooms for role-playing any type of sexual or intimate needs you could think up, but he didn't want that; a fertile playground for many things.

He wanted a woman to talk to, someone local.

He sat there, looking at the damn screen, eyes going blurry as he thought about the possibility of finding someone in the small town he lived in. He knew that someone in this shithole town just had to be in a local chat room. He started clicking through the rooms, and soon found a user created room under his state that had a room with about a hundred people in it from his town. He clicked into the room. He saw a lot of names that didn't strike his fancy, but sat and watched as the conversation went from the local government having to shut down the only elementary school in his town, to a car accident that happened during rush hour traffic.

He hovered his mouse over the names on the right side, and read the brief comments and info that popped up. He started looking for a woman to IM after that, and sorted the users by sex. Half of them would probably be guys looking for a funny story to tell; some would be cops looking for perverts. He wasn't one, and respected the cops who spent hours trolling websites for that one person who was dumb enough to go for the dark stuff.

He didn't see any promising names or conversation going on in the room, so he logged off and went to bed.

She saw his username pop into the room, and noticed he stuck around for about a half hour, not saying anything. His username was unusual, it was a name she'd heard before when she was a teenager and deeply involved in magic and paganism. He logged off, but she still had the private message box open so sent him a brief message.

Your name, it's an old god's name. Did you know that?

She sent it, and then logged off before she could regret it.

The next day, he skipped logging in and checking out the chat rooms. He had too much work to do, and he was tired once it was done. He was hungry for something to stimulate him sexually, but he also wanted someone to talk to him. He was single, and while he needed sex, and even craved it, he wanted more. He wasn't sure what it was he wanted, or needed, beyond that so let himself drift off.

She logged in; not seeing his name or a reply made her nervous. Biting her lower lip, she sent another message to him.

I'm sorry if I bothered you. Your profile pic is of you, right?

She sent it, but this time she waited and held a few conversations while she researched something she had been curious about for a while. She was looking up tulpas, and what it would take to make one. She felt that ache, the building in her groin of needing something, anything to stimulate her. She started rubbing her groin across the seat of the chair, stimulating herself. She stopped typing in the chat room and closed her eyes as she came. She slid off the chair, and into the bathroom, cleaning up and slipping into fresh underwear and pants.

She went back to the computer and started researching more into tulpas. She kept reading and getting more and more excited, because a simple tulpa could be made in a few weeks, especially for what she wanted. Tulpas were your thoughts came to life, created by the energy of your mind focusing so heavily on the object you desired. All she wanted was a simple male form, nothing fancy.

It shouldn't be too hard, right?

She put the idea aside for a moment, checking the chat one more time before going to bed. She started to worry that she frightened him off or something.

He logged on before work and found two private messages waiting for him. He sat there, having to leave for work in less than fifteen minutes. He decided to reply from an app on his phone, he had forgotten until now. Whoops.

Been busy, I'll answer later today on lunch break. :-D

She checked before work and saw his message. She squealed in delight and got dressed. She wanted to see what would happen with Daemos when he replied. Curious to see where he picked up the username, she was dancing around her bedroom and the living room. She spent the morning cleaning and singing songs to herself, favorites from her teens.

She jumped when her computer dinged. It was Daemos' reply.

Yeah, Daemos is the god of love, true love. That's my ugly mug on my profile.

She replied to him and a conversation started.

You're not ugly. You piqued my interest the other night, but you left before I could talk to you. What're you looking for? Conversation? Similar interests?

Sex. Love. Something to make me smile. I live alone, and I don't have anyone to talk to. You live in Hansburg right?

What do you mean sex? Just fucking and leaving, or more? I don't want banged, I need a connection. Please, be the connection I need, she thought.

More. I want to have a conversation with someone afterwards. Video games, the paranormal, news, politics. Something!

Me too. What do you want in a girl? Oh wow! He wants things I want!

:-/ trying to see if I'm a dick looking for a thin woman with big boobies, eh?

No! I want to know if this is what you want.

She took a risk and sent a picture of a couple having sex; no thrills, but enjoying themselves.

He saw the picture pop up on his phone, and he smiled. This woman wasn't shy, and maybe she wouldn't mind a little strangeness. He sent a picture that was saved on his phone. It was of a woman who was standing over a man who had a blind fold on. The woman had his cock in her left hand, and her right hand in a nice grip on his left nipple.

A little bit like this.

She smiled, and sent a picture back to him of a man taking a woman from behind; his hands between her legs, pleasuring her with his fingers as he fucked her. Her head was turned back at him, a large O of a mouth. Her hair was long and covered her breasts, but she looked like she was gasping in pleasure.

:-) I like that, it's hot. What else you like?

She wasn't sure where to go with this, but she sent the emoticon for a shy smile.

It's ok... You can tell me. Right now I'm not anyone you know, or have known, or maybe even will know. Strangers can make the best people to reveal things to. Your choice.

I... have a crazy idea, but I don't know if you'd be into it. Its stranger than just a threesome or banging in public. I want something that can be male or female when I want it to change... To sleep with me...

How do you plan on doing that? Why not just have a threesome?

Because... I want what I want then and there, not having to switch partners. If I want cock, I want it then. If I want pussy while sucking cock, I want it to change instantly. My needs change on a whim, I...

Are you a woman whose needs are like the wind?

Actually, yeah. I am. But I'm not the type to fuck and run. I can't, and it's been done to me too many times.

He sat there, staring at his phone. He felt a connection building. He felt the same way, and he was suddenly honest.

To many times I've done that. Fucked and run. I'm tired, so fucking tired of it. I need someone, even if it's just for a few years. I don't know. I just need someone.

Sitting at her computer, her heart leapt. He was being honest, brutally honest, and she respected that.

Me too. For too long I've just floated through my life. Living, working, playing around.

They sat there for a few seconds in digital silence. His avatar revealed he was typing a long comment.

So. This is kind of a neat idea. How do you plan on doing this? Tulpa or something that you create? I've looked into them before and they're as real as you and me. More real in some ways, though if you lose control of it, the thing can be dangerous. A poppet might be a better idea, a wax one. More of a sex doll, only it does what you tell it to.

She considered the poppet idea for a minute, and she then noticed he was typing again.

Maybe you could meet with me for dinner and we can decide

how to do this.

Her heart jumped more this time, and she wasn't sure how to respond even though she only had milliseconds to do so.

Yes, when?

Tonight at McDonalds, ok? I'll buy if you show up. I'll be wearing a shirt that has a monkey on it saying a funny message. You'll know it's me from the profile picture too. We'll sit and talk.

She fired back her cell phone number and her real name. She was terrified that he'd back out, but said she'd meet him at seven when she got off from work. She sent a basic picture of herself to his cell phone after he sent his number. His reply was a smiley and thumbs up icon. She giggled, and tried to focus for the rest of the day.

He sat at the main entrance, nibbling on a parfait and waiting. It was ten after seven and he was worried he'd fucked up. He felt the tap on his shoulder, and turned around. He smiled as he saw her standing there in front of him. She was exactly as the picture showed. He stood up and offered his hand, introducing himself. She kept glancing at him; his eyes, his hair, his slight tummy. She was talking, but all he could was her dark green eyes, and her moving lips. He started walking to the counter, and she followed.

His hearing came back when he touched her hand by accident as he turned to ask what she wanted.

"I hope you don't think I'm crazy. It's just an interesting idea I had one night. Well, for a lot of nights," she said. She had been talking but he kept just standing there in awe of her.

"It's interesting. I don't deal with that stuff much anymore."

He replied "But I remember a lot from my early teens. What you want? I'm snagging a salad and a coffee. Have whatever you want. I don't judge. Hell, I love it when a woman will *eat* like a person should. Fuck this skinny bitch stuff."

"Uh… you sure?"

"Yep. Whatever you want."

"Fuck."

"They don't serve that here. That might come later."

"Oh my god – I…"

"Spoke your mind," he chuckled as he said it. They were three customers from the counter, and he laughed.

"What?!"

"You're cute. Beautiful."

"Three double cheeseburgers, and I'm gonna go sit down."

She walked off, more of a scurry than a walk, and found the farthest booth from anyone else. She couldn't believe that she'd just said that. She wanted to take him to bed, but hadn't meant to say it. He came back in a bit, a tray of food for him and for her. He set her food down before sitting and setting his own down. He handed her a couple of napkins, and opened his salad container.

They ate in silence. He was feeling the urge for a smoke, but didn't know if she smoked or not. He looked at his watch as she came back from throwing the trash away. She sat down in the booth next to him. Her hand was on his thigh before he could twitch his leg. She kissed his cheek, and squeezed.

"My car is on the other side of the building. You get yours, and I'll wait outside mine. Follow me."

She slid out of the booth, and started for the opposite doorway from where they were sitting. He jumped up, pulling his smokes from his pocket and lighting one even before he got out the door. He jumped in his car and fired the engine up. His hands were shaking, and he didn't know what she had planned. He backed out and pulled around. He saw her smoking a cigarette, as she hopped in her car. It was early summer, so he rolled the windows down. The sun was going to set in an hour and he was curious where they were going. She backed out and he followed behind her.

He kept seeing his hands on her body, cupping her breasts while he held her from behind, their naked bodies pressing against each other; her skin cool and soft, his hands running up and down her sides. She pulled out to the right, and started heading out of town. She gave him plenty enough warning when she turned her left blinker on and turned onto a dirt road. He had a vague idea where she was going, but he kept his eyes on her car. They drove with her leading for another fifteen minutes, until she signaled at what looked like a forest. She slowed down and pulled into a dirt lane. He followed her in. On his left was the thick growth of an old forest, and on his right were miles of pine trees.

He knew this spot well, it was Spirit Woods. The local pagans had bought the land from an old farmer as an area for them to practice their craft. She stopped the car and got out. He stopped too, and leaned his head out the window, as she popped her trunk. She pulled a thick blanket out and slammed her trunk closed. He turned off his engine and got out. He slipped next to her as she walked towards the pine trees.

A thick blanket of old needles coverd the ground and he could smell the sap. She kept on walking in silence and he was quiet, waiting to see what happened. She finally came to a spot and laid the blanket down. She kicked off her shoes and stepped on the blanket, spinning a few times with her arms out. He walked over, took off his shoes too, and stood on the opposite side of the blanket.

She slid off her shirt, her breasts still covered by a skull and cross bone bra. She slipped this off, and he didn't know what the hell to do. She beckoned him closer, and he walked towards her. She motioned for his shirt to come off. He slid it off, and became self conscious. He wasn't overweight, but he had a tummy. She stepped onto the blanket and grabbed his hands.

She pulled him to her and soon they were both on their

knees. His shirt was off, and her hands were sliding down his chest to his belt buckle. He took her soft hands in his, and leaned forward and kissed her. She responded by flicking her tongue into his mouth, and he pulled back.

"People say spirits come out here at night. Something does, I've been here at night and seen some stuff."

"We all have, silly bear. Why else do you think I want to sleep with you here, at dusk? Want to see if something happens?"

"Sure. I'm kinda scared, but…"

"I've put a circle up to keep negative spirits out. If anything enters it'll be ok. Just go with the flow, and let whatever happens happen. Ok?"

He nodded his head and leaned down to kiss her left nipple. She leaned back to give him the room to do so, and started unbuckling his shorts. He let her slide them off, the warm night breeze stirring his body hair and makinggoose bumps appear on his skin. She giggled as she felt it on his arms, and he had her lean back, spreading her legs. He started spreading her labia and as she pointed his tongue to the right spot, he started concentrating there. She soon had her hands in his hair, gasping.

His ass is in the air and his tongue is lapping at her when he sees something in the growing dark. He only caught it from the corner of his eye, a white shimmer. He glanced over and she whimpered as he pulled away. He goes back, but started to feel a warm hand on his right ass cheek, and then the warm hand cupped his cock and balls.

He jumped, unsure of who or what this was, but he relaxed slowly as it started stroking him and playing with his nipples. The left hand moved from his nipples to his ass, a soft finger inserting itself into him. He played with his butt before, but no one else ever had. He twitched and stopped when his lover's legs clamped around his head as she came. She pressed his face into her groin harder and he slipped his tongue inside her, his right pointer finger slipping to her ass, and his left middle finger slid inside her pussy.

He gasped as he felt two of the strange fingers slipping into his own relaxing ass. He lifts his head and looked back, and some form or figure was standing behind him. He felt the hand stroking his cock and the two fingers are tapped a rhythm that makes him start pouring pre-come. He spread his legs, now on his hands and knees to allow it full access to him. He came hard and the hands pulled away from him as he sat on his butt. She's staring at him, eyes flicking between her and the tulpa that had been pleasuring him.

His hands in hers, she started showing where she wanted to be touched, which was everywhere. She turned around and pressed her ass against him, his hard-on pressing into her ass. The entity reached out to her pussy, fingering her as she started to lower herself onto her lover's hard-on. They moved into a sitting position, with him lying down after a few seconds. He didn't know what exactly was going on, but he wanted to see where it went.

Her eyes are clenched shut, she's focusing on the tulpa and her needsd from him, and the moment was still.

Sitting on his lap, his cock in her, and she started gyrating back and forth, her ass gripping tighter as she came close to coming, the wax like hand playing with her clit. A second hand started stroking her face, and she senses and tastes the tuplas strange dick on her lips. The lukewarm material or substitute for flesh twitched running across her lips for her to open. She smells something similar to ozone from it, and she slowly opened her mouth. Taking it in her right hand she starts bobbing, but it kept trying to go deeper into her mouth. Wrapping her hands around the buttocks of the being in her mouth, and she dug her nails into its buttocks. When her nails sunk into it and it didn't react, she loosened her grip of the strange flesh.

He has been looking around her at the creation, and it is

the facsimile of a man, generic in form. Wanting to try something he reached forward, stroking the cock in her mouth. She pulled back enough for him to grip and start masturbating it. She started swirling her tongue around the dripping head, slipping her tongue into the urethra opening. The cock in her mouth started coming and she feels it pulse, her lover pulling his hand away. The fluid is tasteless, but thick like a gravy. She gripped the cock with her left hand and swallowed the two loads of come it squirted into her mouth. It pulled away, and her own orgasm builds, her groin on fire as she came. The heat started in her groin and reached to her chest. She moaned loudly as the orgasms rolled through her, like waves of heat.

She slid off of her lover, turning and pushing him down. She slid on top, pressing her breasts into his face, and he started sucking and squeezing, pinching her nipples harder as she slipped him into her. Her back, sides, neck, face, ass and breasts are being stroked and stimulated as his soft finger tips explored her. She giggled and his smile is visible in the dark.

She started rolling her hips, pounding and thrusting against his groin, her breath escaped her in sharp yips of pleasure. He arched back and turned his head side to side in bliss and pleasure. Hands on her hips, his eyes closed he feels a need. He wanted it in his mouth, to go down on it. She's riding him harder and they were moaning in pleasure, when the tulpa moved closer.

He saw the cock there in front of him, and took it into his mouth. He'd never sucked on a cock before, but he covered his teeth with his lips and started to bob back and forth, his tongue feeling for the heat of the flesh. His right hand snaked down to his lover's clit, and he started stroking her as he grips the cock with his mouth, getting a rhythm going. He pulled it from his mouth, sucking on the balls and lower shaft, slipping it back into his mouth. The testicles of the thing are like plastic, and the tupla has no definitive smell. He was puzzled by the lack of smell or taste to it, but he was lost in the moment.

In seconds it came and is disengaging its member from his mouth. He felt like he did something wrong, but a hand caressed his face. He smiled and then his lover was laying on him, legs spread wide while still riding him. As the couple are lost in a moment of pleasure and orgasm, the tulpa moved in close behind her. They slow, turning and looking at the creature. It puts the shapes of hands on his, and positioned behind her. She leaned forward, kissing him hard on the lips, and bit his shoulder.

They both feel the entities cock enter her ass, and for a moment she doesn't move. Warm legs are intertwined with the two human lovers' and she felt the hands on her breasts. She thrusted backwards a little, and the third lover starts thrusting, hard and fast. The two humans stay still, feeling the hard, fast strokes of the entity. They both made sounds of pleasure as the entity fucked both of them; she finding a rhythm where she's fucking both male lovers. Her human lover gripped her hips, and starts thrusting between the spaces of time her other lover wasn't. It's a rhythm they three keep for awhile, till she started to feel her orgasm blossom. He hold off as long as possible, but her moans and grunts pushed him over the edge. He came inside her, head and back arching, and she squeezed his cock as she came twice in quick succession.

They both felt the entity pull out of her ass and they separated. She lay next to him, kissing him and not saying anything. They didn't know what exactly happened, but they relaxed in each other's arms falling asleep in the dark for awhile. They woke up in each other's arms, the blanket wrapped around them.

He slipped between her legs again, licking and playing with her. She came quickly and pulled him up on her. She spread her legs and draped them over his shoulders, and he slipped easily inside her. He looked around for the entity, but it wasn't seen. He felt a quick pang of longing, sad that it left.

He started thrusting hard and fast, and she wrapped her legs around his neck, his hands on her hips. They fucked hard, fast, and came just as hard as before, if not more so with the added intimacy of being alone together. She unwrapped her legs from around his neck, and he leaned back on his haunches.

She sat up, taking his member in her hand, getting him to stand. She took him into her mouth and swallowed him deeply. His was as deep as he could be when she flexed her throat tight around him. He stiffened and gasps, and put his hands in her hair and she started bobbing, wanting him to come quickly. She covered his cock in saliva as she's bobbed and before long he started whispering he was going to come. He was grunting and whispering nonsense as she kept the pace, wanting his orgasm in her mouth. He came, once and his knees were shaking with the expulsion of energy.

He lowered himself with effort to lay next to her, and laid his head on her shoulder. They remained like this for a long while, holding each other in the dark.

Slowly getting dressed they discussed all the things that come to mind, answering quickly and honestly. They held each other in the night, talking until the chill came.

"Favorite color?"

"Burnt orange."

"Favorite foods?"

"Chinese, Mexican, and Mongolian."

"Didn't you hate Mr. Prazton?"

"Yeah I did."

As they made their way back to their cars, using their cell phones as flashlights, it dawned on them both that they wanted to hang out together. It was before 11, and they were both wired. He sat in his car, waiting for her to get in hers. Backing out, she called him on the phone.

"You want something to eat? I've got half a pizza at my

place."

"I've got cold chicken."

"Damn, choices."

"Subs from Wal-Mart?"

"Sure. Your place or mine?"

"If you don't mind cats… mine?"

"You have kitties! A man with cats!"

"Baxter and Draco. Had them for years, and they've been good companions. So, my place?"

She nods, and they both know the direction to the store to they drive out, not following each other.

They drive, him taking time to get to the parking lot. In the parking lot, they walk hand in hand into the store. Talking about everything they want, oblivious to the world around them, they move forward. The conversation lasted until the late of night, and into the early morning.

When they finally woke up the next day, it was the relaxed silence of couples that had been together for years, not awkward or convoluted. It felt normal, and they realized that they made a connection.

He sat there, looking at her over a cup of tea. They were discussing games they loved as kids, and he couldn't stop staring at her. He was speaking, but his mind was going a thousand miles a minute.

Is this it? Are we doing something permanent here? Fuck it. I want this. I need this.

Unknown to him, she was on autopilot too, thinking nearly the same thing. They suddenly stopped talking, and laughed together. It was the shared laughter of two people who had been buried for too long, hidden for far longer than expected. They let it roll, let it come.

After the laughter came tears, and after the tears came cuddling. Connections were made, bonds formed. Thoughts and words kept internal for too long took shape, became real. Before they knew it, it was late.

"Jenny, can you come back tomorrow? I'm off after-"

"Yeah, I'll be here. Six, right?"

He nodded, scared and excited. He wanted her to come back, wanted her to stay.

She came back.

Moon Bath

My wife Nancy loves to moon bathe nude and it has never bothered me, not even when she first brought it up. I went and got her a mesh tent, got it set it up and everything because she didn't need to be eaten alive by the insects. We lived in the country, in the middle of Arkansas then. During the summer, after the kids had gone to bed and the moon was in the sky, she'd slip outside in her silky robe, nude underneath. She'd set up a small candle, usually scented, and would lie in the moonlight for a few hours. Our office was on the first floor, and the computer sat in front of the large picture window facing her. I'd slip off and play games or work on my novel while she did that, and keep an eye out for her. We had wild animals in the woods surrounding our property, but nothing bigger than a deer or two so, I wasn't concerned, and I could see her if I turned off the light in my room, and watch her in the candle light of the tent. She'd lie out there on the lawn chair, sometimes sleeping; sometimes she'd masturbating if she knew I was watching.

I always enjoyed her little shows, sometimes beating off with her. She never mentioned it, and neither did I. We had been married for twelve years when the incident occurred. I had been worried about Bigfoot or some paranormal monster charging out of the woods at first, but as the years went by and nothing happened, I relaxed. There were a few times while I was out hiking, alone or with the family when I'd seen things. Sometimes it was an out of place animal, or the fleeting shadows dancing in strange ways, but sometimes not so I always kept it to myself. I still kept an eye on her out of curiosity and watchfulness.

It was a simple quirk that Nancy had, and it was safe. Sometimes when she came in she was hungry for me, and we took advantage of it like we normally did if the timing and moods were right.

Then something happened one night, and to this day I still can't figure out what it was. She was lying on her stomach when two forms came walking out of the woods, a light pale shape which turned out to be light, pale shapes of two nude men. I freaked out and jumped up, but when they walked up to the tent she turned over and waved them in. Curious, I sat down and slid the chair over to see better. I had the lights off, and I turned off the monitor then too. Sitting in the dark, I felt my stomach start to wobble, but something excited me about this encounter. She sat up, sitting cross legged on the chair. It wobbled, and she steadied herself, and then the two figures stood before her. For a few minutes she sat there, and then she started nodding. The one on the left walked closer to her as she reached out for him. In the light of the moon, the shape seemed to glow and as it walked closer, I could make out a penis, growing hard with each step. When he was but a few feet from her, it stood out, erect and bobbing slightly.

She reached out and started stroking it, and he moved closer. Leaning down, she kept stroking it while she took the tip into her mouth, bobbing up and down slowly. The other figure walked closer, and his erection looked like a glow stick bobbing in the air. She took it in her other hand and as she stroked and sucked both of them, I grew hard myself.

I had fantasies about seeing my wife with other people, women and men, but I never mentioned them. These things were alien and scary to me, but were touching her now. Their hands caressed her breasts, her shoulders, all along her jaw line. Sitting there watching as her bobbing increased, I felt a pang of jealousy, but my arousal took me by surprise. My nipples hardened under my shirt, and my erection was hot and thicker than normal, pressed against my thigh in my jeans. I shifted in the seat, trying to get the hot flesh off my thigh, but the jeans were too tight. I sat there, watching.

She switched to the other figure, swallowing his hard-on deeper than the other, still stroking the first one. Suddenly she stood, and my heart leapt. I was worried she was freaking out, but then I noticed what she was doing. She folded the chair and slid it to a corner, sitting on her knees while she blew the second figure. The first figure moved behind her, and I could tell he was playing with her breasts and maybe clit. She pulled herself away from the second figure and exposed her neck. She was aroused; I knew this movement from her. She wiggled her hips a little in excitement and spread her legs a little more. The figure behind her started kissing her neck and she reached back, cupping his balls.

In the light of the full moon I could see everything, and my vision was like a hawk's. I seemed to be able to see a bit better when I focused, and looked closer at her. The soft, pale flesh of the figures stood out against her lightly tanned skin, and her dark black hair was up in a bun. Her fingers contrasted against the pale flesh of the thing. I wasn't sure what they were, but I wanted to watch them take my wife. She seemed to enjoy the attention she was getting. The first figure slid behind her and started playing with her ass, as the second leaned down to suck on her nipples.

Her breasts were a medium C with long nipples. I loved to play with them and stare at her cleavage as she would lie in bed next to me. She started running her hands over the second figure in front of her, scratching his chest as the rubbing on her ass continued. She didn't normally like anal, but when she did, we both had fun.

I couldn't stand the growing heat against my thigh anymore, so I stood up quietly, unzipping my jeans and pulling myself free. My cock was hot and thick in my hands, slick with pre-cum. I started stroking soft and slow not wanting to come yet.

As I stroked, the figure behind her sat on the ground, legs stretched before him, as he lifted her with his hands. My wife was a bit heavy, and it shocked me to see him just lift her like a paperweight. He slowly lowered her ass onto his erect cock, and she slid down to the base. Her hands were on the mesh floor, balancing herself, when she started bouncing and leaning back. He started kissing her neck and shoulders while his hand slid to her waist. The second figure came over and started stroking in front of her, a few feet away. Her bouncing increased and the strokes of the second figure did too. Suddenly it stiffened, and I knew he had come on her because she started running her hands over her chest and stomach in a rubbing motion. I came suddenly, unaware that I was that close.

She slid off of her lover and lay on her side, facing the figures. She was gesturing to the two forms and they moved closer. They started kissing and touching each other, hands on each other's chests, necks, and cocks. The first figure kneeled down, and took the other in his mouth. I stood there, turned on by this new event. As the first figure bobbed quickly, I started stroking again faster than before. The second figure stiffened, running his hands over the seemingly bald head of the first. My wife got behind the first figure, playing with his ass. Her middle finger slipped easily into it, and it was on all fours suddenly. The second figure stood there, watching. As the first figure orgasmed, I did too. I was sticky with my own semen, and I started pinching my nipples with my free left hand.

The second figure sat down, then stretched out, beckoning my wife over. She slid atop, and I saw its pale cock slip inside her. She started thrusting fast and hard, hands on its chest as she fucked it. I was still hard and stroking, something that hadn't happened in a long time. My breathing was rapid and shallow, my arousal exhilarating and terrifying at the same time. The first figure slipped himself into my wife's ass and she leaned against it. If the window had been open, I would have been able to hear her moans of pleasure. Riding the thing under her, she allowed the thing in her ass to pound into her. Her hands went to her breasts, squeezing and pinching her long nipples. Suddenly, she froze, hands on the ground. I swear I heard a yelp of pleasure as she came, even through the windows. Slowly the beings slid free of her, standing in front of her. They leaned down, the second figure first kissing her, then the other. She was still on her hands and knees and her head dropped to the floor of the tent. The two figures slowly walked out.

They waved at her prone form, then in my shock, turned to face me. They waved, and headed into the woods. I stood there, and I felt terror and arousal like I had never before.

Suddenly I found myself outside, unzipping the tent and stepping in before I could think. My wife was still in that position, and I was nude too. I crawled across the tent floor to her and when I was right behind her, I leaned forward, licking her ass followed by her wet slit. She knew it was me, because she moaned my name. I shushed her, and started licking the outer edges of her ass. I wanted her, wanted to taste her and her strange lovers. I was preternaturally hard, and I wanted in her too.

Licking her ass while I played with her breasts from behind, I felt her orgasm build. She squirted suddenly, her legs shaking and the gasp from her loud. I started licking her slit, sucking on the outer lips as she stroked herself. I tasted a strange seed and swallowed it willingly. Her next orgasm was smaller, but I wanted in her. I got on my knees behind her and slipped myself inside. My hands went to her hips and she started thrusting back, moaning my name. My pounding brought me to a quick orgasm, rocking both of us forward. I pulled out of her slowly, rubbing my head across her outer lips. She rolled over, coated in sweat and stared into my eyes. I smiled brightly in the dark, and she did too. I raised my pointer finger to my lips, telling her to be quiet. As I kneeled there panting, she snaked over to her robe, and slipped it on. She walked to me on wobbly legs, leaning down. She kissed me hard and long, her mouth tasting of the strange semen she'd swallowed. I was aroused again, but she was done for the night. I let her slip into the house and saw the small bathroom light cast a square patch on the grass on the right side of as I sat there, nude in the warm night.

I felt strange, but knew that this wasn't a bad encounter she and I had experienced. If anything it meant that we had something special occur. I knew about the strange things in the woods where we lived, and I knew this was something paranormal that no one would ever be able to explain or even understand, so I stood on my own wobbly legs and quickly ran into the house upstairs to our bedroom.

I ended up dressing and laying next to my wife, passing out almost instantly that night. We've never discussed it. There are times when she goes out to moon bathe and comes in a little disappointed. I know that if they were to come back, even after we've moved... I'd want to join in, experiencing my wife with the figure or beings that slept with her.

I keep thinking off and on about the things and what they were. Maybe my wife created tulpas, thought beings made flesh and blood but if that were true, that would mean that she had been wanting that type of encounter for awhile, putting many nights of thought into it. I had been researching them about a year before the incident, talking about them to Nancy. I was sitting at the table getting ready to start my new story idea when I brought up the idea of something coming to life, just by thinking about it long enough and putting enough willpower into it. She just stared at me, across the table, and nodded silently. I always thought that the idea went over her head, or she didn't understand what a tulpa was.

As I think back to it, she went out nearly every night she could after that, and until the beings showed up. I haven't asked her about my suspicions, but I think Nancy thought those things into existence. I've wanted to ask her if she wanted to bring them back, or if it was a one-time experience but as I watch her, several years later, I feel as if something may come back soon. It might only be one of them, maybe both. As she comes in, looking bummed out, we curl up together; sometimes making love, other times just laying there until we pass out.

I think if I can, I might create my own tulpa for us. When she goes out, I will start focusing on one. If Nancy can do it without much knowledge of the supernatural, I should be able to easily, but as I work on it, I will bring it up to her, speak of it finally. It was strange, exhilarating, and unique that night. While the magic isn't gone from our marriage, a little more magic would be neat too.

DANNY BOY

Danny walked with a purpose through the crowded streets; he was looking for a mark, a target. He had the picture of her burned into the back of his eyes, from staring at it in the hotel room he had rented in the crappy section of town. The rundown hotel took only cash, and the few mice in the place scurried under the dresser that was bolted to the floor as he entered the room. He just needed a home base while he searched for the best method of eliminating the target. He didn't have a name, just a picture. He sat there, hours upon hours on the edge of the bed, memorizing as much as he could of her face.

It looked like a corporate picture, she was wearing a suit. The woman had bright red hair that was cut close, a pixie cut. Her eyes were a dark color, and there was a small scar on her right eyebrow, about two inches long, going vertically. The scar continued under her right eye by a few centimeters. It didn't make her less attractive, if anything it made him curious about her.

Danny shoved the curiosity into a dark corner of his mind, because when he got curious he got hurt. A few marks ago, he learned that lesson. He had been out of the game for several years because of it. Getting close meant pain, and he was tired of hurting. He stood, startling the mice that gathered around his feet. His knees popped, and he turned towards his two backpacks. He unzipped one and pulled a wallet out, a small handgun and a knife. He slipped them into the respective spots. The gun went under his left armpit in a holster he had made by hand, and the knife had a hip sheath he strapped onto a belt loop. He looked at the mice and waved goodbye.

Now he was in the center of downtown Cleveland at two in the morning. He had tracked her down from the application on his phone, a burner that he picked up a few hours earlier. Uploading her photo into the phone allowed him to send the app for a search in Cleveland as to where she might be. It pinged several likely places for him to try, and from them he headed off to Ziggy's. The club was a strange place full of BDSM practitioners. When he walked in he saw a table with three men and a woman, a black bag on the table. He walked past, scanning for the target. She wasn't on the dance floor, or anywhere he could see. There were private rooms upstairs, but he wasn't going to blow his cover by searching them. When he went to a bartender and flashed her picture, he got bad news.

"Yeah, she stopped coming here about six months or so ago. She and her girlfriend got into a huge fight one night in a private room. We decided not to let her back in. Her girlfriend stopped coming here too. I miss 'em, they lit up the place."

The bartender sputtered this quickly while mixing several drinks at a time. Danny pulled the phone from his pocket and checked off Ziggy's. Walking out, he started following the directions to the second place, a bar three blocks over. He lit a smoke as he walked, flicking the ashes on the concrete. When he finished the smoke, he made sure to drop it right into the sewer drain.

He stepped into the doorway of the bar and saw her in the back, under a neon light advertising beer. He slid up to the bar and, ordered a light cocktail, and paid cash. He pulled his phone out and started texting. The bot program responded to him, and he kept typing random things while keeping an eye on the target. She had several bottles on her table, and when she walked to the restroom she was wobbly.

Danny left his drink there, went outside and crossed the street. The bartender had been in the kitchen when he left, and Danny could see him from his hiding spot. Between two businesses there was a small enough crack in the dark for him to hide in. He stood there, waiting patiently. He pulled the handgun from his lower back, the holster warm from his flesh. The woman walked out, phone to her ear.

As he raised the gun to fire, he heard someone screaming his name.

"Danny! What the fuck?"

"What the fuck are you doing? Jesus he's doing it again Martha!"

Danny was standing in the middle of the living room, nude, and he woke up almost instantly. He blinked a few times and sprinted for his bedroom.

Holy fuck! I did it again. I hope to god Martha and Bill don't kick me out. Oh god.

He sat on the edge of the bed, looking around the room. The night air was hot and stuffy in his room, and he realized that the air conditioner had been turned off. He didn't know if he been the one to do it or not. He had been here for several years, and had only done this one other time unwittingly. He had been thinking of walking in a cold rain, it pouring down. The next thing he knew, he was standing in the kitchen when hundreds of gallons of water appeared over him and flooded the house.

He was a dream weaver. He could turn any dream he was having into a reality, but until recently he'd never used it for himself. He was shaking, and there was a small knock on his door. He jumped, terrified to open it. He stood slowly, and cracked the door.

"Danny, hey. You ok man?" Bill was nervous to ask him anything. What did they see?

"Yeah. I need to sleep. I've been doing too much stuff lately with you guys."

"You had a gun. We didn't know what you were going to do. It happened again, and that never happens, does it?"

Danny shook his head and closed the door. He sat down on the bed again, and a memory came to him. It was of his foster parents, his second actually. He remembered being angry at the first foster parents, but not why he ended up with the Grants. He would never forget them or the love they gave him. This was before Dad figured out what Danny could do.

Danny boy! You're going to make some lady or dude so happy one day! You gotta keep this secret though, people will hurt you. You make dreams come true, like a dream weaver.

He had never used his skill for anything bad, only to make people happy. It didn't change his life all that much. He was able to hold regular jobs, and he had until about a year ago when he woke up tired of being a cook at a hospital. Figuring he needed a change of scene, he just started driving across the state. Starting from Cleveland, he worked his way all the way to Cincinnati over the course of a month. He found a job as a janitor in a school, and cleaned there for several months until he got bored of living in the big city. Then he found this small town about a hundred miles east. He landed in it because his car just up and died, the engine blowing.

He called his dad that day, telling him that he was ok but the car was dead.

"Danny boy, you need some money?"

"No Dad, I'm fine out here. I have a job already; it's working behind the counter of a gas station. I think I have a place above the garage here. I'll send you an email on what all is going on when I get to a connection." He glanced at his laptop case, knowing full well that the only place that would have wifi he could connect to was the library.

He hung up the phone and went to work. He had been working in the gas station for several weeks when Martha and Bill came in. They were a couple in their late forties, and they looked grumpy. They might have had life before, but now everything looked grey to them.

"Hey guys! Anything I can help you with?"

"No, buddy. Unless you guys have a thirty pack of Bud Light, we'll just get this." The man plopped down a twelve pack and asked for a carton of smokes. Danny turned and got them, when he turned around he had a big smile on his face.

"You two need something fun, don't you?"

The couple stood staring at him, unsure if he was being serious or being an asshole. The man cleared his throat.

"No, seriously. You guys need some fun. Tell you what, I get off at seven tonight. How about you two come back here, mostly sober and we can have some fun. Good clean fun."

The couple looked at each other and the man slid his card through the reader near him. It wouldn't work, so Danny took the card to swipe it on his side. He glanced at the name on the card, noticing that both of them were listed on it. He ran the card and it went through, taking several minutes. The customers, Bill and Martha, seemed nervous about the card not working, and sighed in relief when the printer gave them a receipt. They grabbed the booze and the cigarettes and almost bolted out the door. He watched them climb into a beat to hell pickup truck before they drove off in a tail of dust.

He worked the next two hours, almost forgetting about them until they pulled back into the parking lot around six fifty or so. He smiled to himself, rubbing his hands together. It had been a long time since he made anyone happy with his skill, and he was hoping he could tonight.

He switched the gas station over to the night clerk and walked out. He lit a smoke and walked over to the truck. It was her, Martha, in the driver seat. He walked over to the passenger side door and hopped in.

"Where's the hubby?"

"Home. Can you really give us a good time? It's been such a long time…"

"Yep! You or both of you?"

"I want Bill to –" She started crying, leaning into the steering wheel and sobbing. Danny reaches over, putting his hand on her shoulder. She tried to shrug it off, her dry skin not liking the smooth skin of his hand. He holds on a bit tighter, and it came to him.

Bill and Martha are sad. Lonely together, they sit and watch the same DVDs and movies over and over. He works just enough to pay the rent and to get by. They both pass out in the recliners in the living room. Sometimes from boredom, sometimes its booze, but always because they don't want to face reality.

Danny feels bad for them, but he also knows how he can help.

"I know, I do. You need him to be happy so you can be. I can make it happen. I'll show you if you take me home. Ok?"

She turns and stares at him, a thousand things pouring through her head and heart. She doesn't want to believe him, but she *does.* There is an honesty and respect in this strange man. His short grey hair is basic, and he's six feet tall with a big belly in front of him and the goofiest bug eyes she's ever seen. He doesn't look handsome at all to her. She shrugs, fires the truck up, and backs out of the parking spot.

They ride in silence, the radio long busted on them. The dirt roads seem to last forever, then they pull up in front of a single story house. It's more like a brick; squat and starkly white against the green of the yard. The truck is turned off and in the front lawn is Bill, laying stomach down on the grass. Martha walks over to him, kicking him once in the gut.

Bill stirs, looking up at Danny and Martha with red eyes. He isn't sure what he thinks, so he stumbles to his feet. "You day guy who say he can make us sappy!"

Danny nods once. He turns to Martha and looks at the front door. She leads Bill over and beckons Danny in. The house is clean, sad and sparsely furnished; the two recliners and the old TV in the corner, the kitchen with a table, three chairs and the appliances. He walks into the kitchen, grabs the first chair he sees, and drags it to the living room. He sits in it, facing the standing couple.

"Sit. I'll explain how this works, and you decide if you agree."

They plop themselves down, Bill doing his best to listen. Martha is staring at the floor as Danny starts telling them the deal.

"You have to tell me one small fantasy you've had recently. Then, I'm going to go lie down somewhere and sleep."

Bill is angry and indignant, starts muttering under his breath. Martha glares at him and he quiets down. Martha blinks several times, unsure how to answer, or if she should at all.

"That's it? Just tell you our fantasy and you go sleep? Are you touched in the head?"

"Dad says I'm touched by the grace of God. But yes, that's the deal. Yes or no?"

Bill having dosed off, is sleeping in his recliner, and Danny gets up slowly to walk over to him. Danny shakes his leg several times trying to wake him. Bill doesn't stir, and he turns towards Martha who is staring at him intently.

"Can I ask for money? Will I get that?"

"No ma'am, that's against my rules. Everyone wants money, even the richest people do. You have a personal fantasy. What is it?"

To listen, he plops himself in the kitchen chair, crossing his leg. Martha looks at the floor as if she's about to cry again. Danny looks on at her, patient and waiting.

"I wish Bill made love to me. Was sober and in a good enough mood to take his time."

Danny looks at her and nods three times. He stood and looked for the bedroom. She told him in quiet tones, and he motions for her to sit still. He found the bed, pulled off the sheets and comforter. Throwing it into a pile, he climbed onto the bare bed. Lying on his back, he quickly fell asleep.

He awoke several hours later to what he thought were screams of pain. He bolted up, thinking that maybe he fucked up. Then, as he was about to run into the living room, he heard it again. It was Bill, making this loud squeal of pleasure in the living room. Martha was laughing now, and Danny settled back into bed, sleeping deeply after a few minutes. The dream weaving always made him tired for a few days. He should have warned them, but they would be occupied for a few hours if not longer.

When he fully woke up, he found himself in the bare bed. He pulled his phone from his pocket, but it was dead. He sat on the edge of the bed, holding his head in his hands. He didn't hear any sounds from the house and the thick curtains blocked the light, except for a small sliver of bright white on the floor. He stood, popping everywhere, and walked to the bedroom door. He opened the door and looked out into the living room. They were lying on top of a blanket, nude and curled up. He smiles a thousand watt smile, knowing that it worked.

It was strange after that, they asked him to move in and make them fantasies every now and then. He was fine with it, and they eventually started wanting to involve him. He'd never dream weaved with himself in it. It was hard at first, being awake and asleep at the same time. To work up to it he spent weeks on end, training himself in the art of meditation first. He read books and websites to learn different techniques he could use. Eventually, one clicked with him and he was able to meditate while being awake.

Being able to send his consciousness into a place to sleep

while he was awake was next. Being special as he was, what would take other people a lifetime to perfect he was able to do in about a month and a half. He started simple at first, with a focal point. In his mind he could imagine a vast white space, a nothingness that brought him to a state of meditation. The next step was more intensive, but according to the book he was reading, if he could do this he was good.

He created a small garden in his mind, a patch of land in a sea of white. The garden had a row of corn, tomatoes, and green beans. At the south end of the garden was a bench and a full watering can. In his mind he was able to see the plants grow and mature, bringing about the fruit and vegetables. He would keep part of his mind working on growing and watering the plants while he worked or did chores. At night he was able to fully focus on the garden. After a few days, the plants were large and healthy.

When they were ripe, he picked them. Preparing them on a stove in his mind, he was able to enjoy what he had grown in his mind. With this difficult task completed, he took it a step further. His plan was to put part of his mind asleep, the dream weaving part. He was scared it wouldn't work or he'd hurt himself, but he was ready to try.

In the sea of white, he created a bedroom. It was similar to the one he had as a kid. While it was designed with an adult in mind, there were reminders of the good things in his life. A picture of his father saying his nickname, an action figure on the desk, and bookshelves packed to the brim. In this room he sent his subconscious to go lay down. Sitting in his room at Bill and Martha's, he entered a sleep state in his mind's eye. As the internal Danny slept in the bedroom, he was wide awake. Danny imaged a simple shoe falling from the ceiling. As the loafer fell in front of him, he giggled. It was working. He stood up and felt the dream weaved shoe. It was as real as could be and he laughed again. His dream weaving self stirred a little and the shoe seemed to shimmer. He put his subconscious self back to sleep deeper, and it solidified. He'd asked many times what it was like for the people he was dream weaving for to hold or become what they wanted to be for a short amount of time.

Most people just smiled and said it was amazing. They wouldn't go into detail, and now he knew why. It was virtually impossible to explain how real it was to even himself. He threw the shoe against the wall, the thwack loud. He grabbed the shoe and went into the living room. He was slow at first, afraid of losing his ability to walk and dream at the same time, but as he moved he knew it was solid.

Entering the living room, he threw the shoe at Bill. He caught it and looked at Danny funny.

"Danny boy, what the hell?"

"It's not real, watch this!"

In his mind, he woke up his sleeping self and the shoe disappeared from the large hands grasping it. Bill blinked several times, and bent over on the couch to make sure he didn't drop it on the floor.

"Whoa, how are you awake? I thought you had to be asleep to dream weave!"

"Not anymore! I can put a part of my mind to sleep, the dream weaving part, and keep me awake! Cool eh?"

Bill laughed and went running into the bedroom. When he came out, he sat on the couch and told Danny to sit. Danny sat down on the recliner that Bill usually sat in, and looked perplexed.

"Danny, I have an idea. Now that you can be awake, we can kinda pay you back for doing this for us."

"I have free room and board, that's enough for me."

"No, we have something in mind. Let me explain."

Bill explained, and two days later all three of them were

ready to try.

Martha and Bill were supposed to pick him up from the local bar. He went into the bathroom and closed the stall door. Putting his dream weaving self to sleep, he started working. He saw himself changing from him into what Bill and Martha wanted.

After ten minutes he looked down at himself, and he could tell his body had changed. Walking to the mirror, he examined the results. His pale skin was gone, replaced with very dark and exotic African skin; his face was altered too. His strange eyes were gone and the face reflecting back at him was one he would love to have if he'd been able to choose. The strong jaw and rounded forehead were better than his own. His jaw was weak, chin and neck a lump of wobbly flesh. His brow was weak too, curved kind of funny like a frown. The doctors said that it was just the way genetics rolled the dice, but he felt dumb with it, almost like a caveman. Lifting his shirt, he saw the lean and muscular body. Not overly muscled, but enough to have a definition. He smiled to himself when he could see his feet without sucking his stomach in.

He left the bathroom, an honest and profound spring to his steps. He glanced around the bar, and knew that if he could stay like this, he could have anyone here he wanted but, his friends were sitting at a table and he walked right over to them instead. Plopping down in a chair, he looked at Bill and Martha.

"You two look like you're in the mood for some trouble."

"Yes we are. What kind of trouble you have in mind?"

"Let's go to my truck and find out. Come on!"

With the predetermined password sequence completed, they all piled into the truck and headed home.

As Bill was driving down the dark roads, Danny started fondling Martha's breasts through her blouse as his other hand massaged the small of her back. She leans forward and pulls her top off. She's braless, and her bare chest is illuminated by the dashboard lights. Martha and Bill were handsome in a rugged country way, and ever since they started dream weaving and growing closer, years melted off of them. Danny was the first one to notice the changes in them. Bill and Martha were taller than him, both of them six feet or so. He was an even five feet and nine inches himself. He noticed the wrinkles and lines disappearing as they grew closer to him as a friend and each other again. Their skin glowed with a touch of youthfulness that had been missing for years. Martha started feeling better about herself, wearing clothes that she hadn't in a long time. The first time she got dressed up, Bill and Danny noticed almost instantly. They came home from a trip to the store with the crinkling plastic bags to find Martha cooking in the kitchen, wearing jeans and a blouse that showed off her figure. Danny dropped his bags on the table and went into the living room.

The giggles and gasps from both of them as he sat and played a game on the computer made him happy.

Bill started dressing and acting better too, his clothes less loose as he built muscles as he worked the fields by hand. Danny kept an eye on them, and now he was hungry for both of them.

He had relationships in the past, both men and women, but they usually ended badly. He couldn't tell if it was him keeping the dream weaving secret, or just him. It hurt, so he didn't bother with relationships after a while. As the three of them had lived together over a few years, he grew attached to them. He almost brought it up several times, and he knew that they had similar thoughts off and on too, but things worked as they were and they continued without comment.

Now he had Martha's left nipple in his mouth, his left hand massaging her other breast. He suckled gently on her nipple; it was hard in his mouth.

"Bite me," Her voice hissed through clinched teeth. She

was wiggling her hips back and forth as the truck bounced along a dirt road. Bill had gone off the main highway and was going down back roads, glancing at them from the corner of his eye. He kept driving at a steady pace, avoiding the biggest ruts and potholes.

Danny bit down with the pressure he thought she meant. Her hand grabbed the back of his head and she pushed him into her breast. They were large, two of Danny's hands in size. The road moving under them made them bounce and shake, and he was enjoying watching the right one dance. His palm that had been massaging her nipple now lay on her thigh, squeezing off and on. She took that hand and put it on her breast again.

"Harder Danny, bite a bit harder. Pinch too!"

He complies, and she moans loudly in the cab. He feels his cock pressed against his thigh, larger and thicker than his real one. He releases both nipples and reaches down to her skirt. She lifts her ass, pulling the skirt down to her knees. She's wet and Danny can clearly smell her arousal. His hand shoots to her groin, middle and pointer finger exploring. Martha starts kissing him, and he jumps in surprise.

"Put your fingers in me, open me."

He slips his fingers down, feeling the pubic hair against his skin, and he opens her outer folds. She lifts herself again, and spreads her legs. He slips in her, and as they kiss deeper, he finger fucks her. She comes, snapping her legs together to make him stop, and he gets the hint. He stops moving and pulls his hand away, breathing heavily himself, and glances at Bill. The two men glance at each other, and the truck slows. They're along the river, and a turn off for a fishing spot is coming up.

As the truck pulls into the gravel, crunching loudly, Martha is undoing Danny's jeans. She wraps her hand around his thick cock and gasps at the thickness. The hot flesh in her hands, she slips him out just as Bill turns off the truck. Danny leans over to Bill and whispers in his ear.

"Take off your pants."

Bill turns to him and in the fading light of the dashboard, Danny motions with his head to do it. Looking back at Martha, he feels her lips taking him into her mouth. The smooth skin of his dick slides across her lips, and into her. As she leans over to take him in deeper, he gasps himself. Bill is now sitting there with his pants and boxers around his knees, cock hard and bobbing as he watches his wife go down on Danny's special form. He's impressed that he's kept this going, not slipping, but he sees his dream weaving self sleeping soundly.

He takes Bill's cock in his hand, and starts stroking it. The cock is covered in pre-cum, and it lubes Danny's hand as he strokes. Using his right arm for balance on the back of the bench seat, he slowly leans towards Bill. Releasing Bill's cock, he starts to suck on him. Bill's fingers bury themselves in Danny's hair, and he pushes himself deeper into Danny's throat. The cock in his mouth is longer than he imagined. He takes as much as he can, and he times his bobbing with Martha's. In seconds the men are coming, large loads filling Danny and Martha's mouths. They swallow, almost in unison. Martha pulls from Danny first, but he keeps bobbing on Bill. Bills hands are clenching his hair, almost trying to pull him away. The second orgasm from Bill is bigger than the first, and Danny savors the bitterness and musky scent.

Pulling from Bill, he sits up, back barking a little from the strange angle. Martha is fingering herself, watching the men in the moonlight coming in the windshield. Bill glances down at Martha and pops his door, the light not coming on. He realizes that his pants are going to trip him, so he pulls them up as he climbs out. Danny follows and he can hear Martha opening her door with a squeak. As the men climb out, Danny pulls a blanket out from under the bench seat. The three walk past the bed, and Danny and Martha spread the thick blanket on the ground behind the truck. Martha sinks to her knees, and cups her breasts in the moonlight. She's beautiful. The three forms are glowing now, a full moon high above them. The water from the river is silent, and they are alone.

Danny walks over to Bill, and drops his pants and boxers again. Wrapping his arms around Bill's neck, they embrace and kiss. Martha watches, sitting on her legs now, and she's smiling in the dark. Her husband and their dream weaver are making out with a passion she's never seen before. It's strange, but she realizes how turned on Bill is as he sinks to his knees. He takes Danny into his mouth, slow and awkwardly. She crawls over to him, running her hands down his back and over his tight ass.

"Start with your lips baby, just run the cock over your lips."

She reaches around him, gripping Danny's cock in a firm hold. She swirls the tip around Bills mouth, his lips coated in pre-cum.

"Now, make a kiss, and I'll guide you."

With her free hand, she pushes gently on the back of his head. With his pursed lips, he bobs gently on the hot tip, and he gets the idea. Martha relaxes her pushing, but starts to stroke Danny as her husband bobs slowly on him. Danny is moaning in pleasure, and his hands are snaking to his shirt, which he takes off. He starts pinching his nipples as he fights thrusting his hips. Bill is bobbing deeper, and with Martha's strokes at the base of his cock, the sensations are intense. He feels himself slipping in his mind, the subconscious waking up.

As the orgasm rips through him, he snaps his eyes shut, clenching them tight. As he clenches his physical eyes shut, his dream weaving self dissipates. He doesn't care; he just wants to feel the orgasm. As the heat spreads from his groin to his chest, he can feel his body coming back as the dreamed flesh disappears. He opens his eyes slowly, looking down at the couple. They're kissing and running hands over each other as Martha pushes Bill to the ground. The two glance up at him and they smile, teeth shining in the dark. Martha and Bill reach for Danny.

He jumps and gasps a little. They want *him* not just his dream weaved self. He sinks to his knees, a pressure of arousal and excitement gripping his chest. He starts kissing Martha while his hands are caressing Bills chest. He pinches the firm nipples when his fingers caress them, and he starts to touch Martha. His hands caress her shoulders, arms, hands. Using the tips of his fingers, he sweeps up to her shoulders again and he stands. Moving behind her, he starts caressing her back and ass, fingertips only a few centimeters from her flesh. She shivers in the warm air. She's continuing to kiss and stroke Bill hard, his hands fingering her sweet spot. The couple are gasping in pleasure, and Danny is stroking Martha even gentler now.

He removes his hands from her and he starts playing with her ass. His middle finger is probing in a circular motion, and he starts gripping her hip, then breast with his other hand. He's a knuckle deep in her when he feels her relax, and slip Bill inside her. Thrusting gently with his middle finger, he snakes his hand to her breast, and he offers it to Bill. With Martha's nipple between his pointer and middle finger, he feels Bill licking and biting her flesh. As Bill nibbles on the nipple, Danny is thrusting his finger to the second knuckle, and her ass is opening a bit more. He slips the pointer next to the one inside her already, and she gasps and looks back at Danny.

She opens suddenly, and he feels around the blanket. Martha dumped a small bag with items on the blanket on the corner. He finds one, and has it on in seconds. Slipping into her slowly after lubing her and himself up, he's gasping at the sensation.

Bill is deep in her, and the couple are still as they feel what Danny is doing. He slips as deep as he is going to for now into Martha, and they freeze for a few seconds. Bill and Danny can feel each other's dicks, and Danny starts thrusting slowly. The three gasp in pleasure as the sensation feels deliciously naughty. Bill is thrusting in time with Danny now, and the three orgasm quickly. They continue in time, driving Martha into another orgasm that makes her body shake. Danny slips from her as he comes hard himself, wanting to change the condom.

As he's changing the condom, Bill and Martha are coming together, wrapped tightly together. On his knees, he knows he wants Bill somehow. Amazed that the three of them have lasted this long, he feels something shifting. Bill and Martha are shimmering, fading out of reality. The night disappears around him, turning into a bright white light that is blinding him now. He closes his eyes, and the heat hits him. It was warm on the bank of the river, but now the heat is impossibly strong. Sweat is pouring out of his body and he can't open his eyes.

The light is burning through the eyelids he has clenched shut, and suddenly it's gone. There are red spots floating ahead of him when he opens his eyes. The heat is coming from the room he's in, it's sweltering in here. Lying on the bed, he sits up, feeling for a light switch or lamp. The darkness surrounds him, and he stands on wobbly legs. He can't feel a switch or a lamp or anything. The concrete floor is hot too, and he reaches upwards. His fingertips brush the ceiling, and it feels like concrete too.

He panics, afraid that he's been arrested or something. He feels the walls, running his hands to the right, and he feels the door. There isn't a knob on his side, but a latch. He tries it, pushing down several times and pulling. It's stuck or locked, and he runs his hands up and down the door. He finds a slot that swings inwards and he lies down on the concrete. The room is large enough for a cot, and for him to lay down with his legs under it. He felt the walls with his feet as he lay there, when he first came to. His shirt and pants feel like cotton, and he doesn't feel anything in the pockets as he lay on the floor, trying to open the food tray slot.

He slips a fingernail on the right edge and slowly eases it up. Laying his head on the warm concrete, he can see a blue and white tiled floor and another door like his. He jumps as the slot squeals in protest as he pushes it all the way up. Scooting closer to the opening, he gets a better view down the hall both ways. The hallway is long, almost infinite with his viewpoint. Both ways stretch for an impossible distance, and there is a pair of men's shoes walking his way. The feet stop at his door and turn towards it. He hears a jingle of keys, and he jumps up, sitting on the cot. The food slot snaps closed and the keys stop turning the lock. It resumes, a loud metal on metal screech deafening him. Danny closes his eyes, not wanting to be blinded by the hallway light. The thing standing there isn't a man.

The creature is simian, it has wide shoulders, and a monkey like face peering in. The wide frame blocks the doorway, and Danny is terrified.

"What the fuck?" Danny screeches in terror.

The simian starts to chatter like a chimpanzee, but it's clearly a language. Danny sits there, scared. The humanoid reaches in with its large arms and grips Danny by the hand, pulling him out. As the hand pulls him out and his body crosses the doorframe, it changes again.

Danny is lying on his bed in Bill and Martha's spare room, staring at himself. Bill is sitting next to the bed, cell phone in hand. He's speaking quietly into it.

"Yeah he's been unresponsive for several hours, staring at the ceiling. I cannot rouse him, and he's breathing just fine. Ok. I'll be waiting on the porch. Thank you."

Bill stands, phone still pressed to his ear as he walks to the bedroom doorway. Danny zips over to his comatose form, trying to reconnect with his physical body. He tried slamming into himself. He tried pinching himself awake; his form just lay there, staring at the ceiling. His astral form is crying, ethereal tears falling and splashing off of his face. He can't wake up and he can't get back into his body. Time passes, and he is shocked when he see's who Bill was waiting for.

His father and Bill come walking in, silent. The chair next to Danny is filled by his father's frame. Bill stands at the doorway, watching.

"I've been doing some research, Bill. Last few years I decided to figure out what Danny Boy's gift is. It's a blessing and curse. Once every few thousand years, someone is born that makes dreams real. As long as the person sleeping can hold the dream in their mind, it holds. It's a form of breaking reality. Most of the time, I guess, the Catholic Church kidnaps the weaver and stuffs them in the Vatican. About the fifteenth century the church stopped. I think Danny was our millennium's weaver."

Danny turns his spectral form towards Bill, and he's crying softly.

"What happened to him? What did we do?"

"I know you explained to me on the phone what happened, and how it did. I don't think you or Martha did anything wrong. Nor did Danny boy, either. The legends and myths that I read spoke of weavers who dreamed themselves into things like you did. When reality started warping when he was just sleeping, you should have called."

"I – I know. I was afraid, and I kept him from working. We didn't do anything except let him be. He was fine, unless he was sleeping. The last time we could rouse him was when he had the gun. He just slipped into a coma when we got him lying down finally. It's been several days." Bill stared at the still figure on the bed and the shaking man in the chair. He remembered the night, after the events in the truck, and then the gun in the living room later that night. He was scared that night Danny lost his mind and was going to kill himself or all of them. Instead, he was dying inside himself.

"His body is going to die. We can't save him and my dear, dear Danny boy will be gone."

Bill nods, crying streams of tears now, face drenched. Danny's father gets up and hugs him in the doorway.

"His mother passed away several years ago. He and I kept in contact. I knew something was amiss after last Sunday. I just wish you could have called me sooner. Now, we wait."

Danny is floating there, screaming incoherently at his father and boyfriend.

"Hey! I'm here! What the fuck, Dad!"

Before Danny knows what to do, time seems to fast forward. Hours slipped by in minutes, and he realizes that things are going downhill. He decides to leave, to leave his body and family to pass on. As he envisions himself above the world, it is zipping by, but suddenly he sees something strange. As the world fast forwards, other Earths and planets are suddenly overlapping. As he rises into the universe, above everything, he sees.

Hundreds, no thousands of multiple universes are stacking upon each other. All of them existing and moving. Ever forward, ever towards a final death of all. He sees two things in each multiverse as it zips in front of him. A large black spire, different in each universe. An anchor point for something bigger, scarier than he can comprehend. The worlds are all different; some don't even have any life in them. Others don't have humans, or anything that could be seen as humanoid.

As he watches, he feels himself fading. Not just from this universe, but from all of them. His physical body is failing, shutting down bit by bit, but he remains, floating and watching. The corporeal body may die, but his spirit doesn't…

His spiritual form is walking along a garden path, beautiful flowers and plants springing up with each step around him, and a figure waits at the end of the lane. As he steps closer his mother is waiting for him, and he runs the last ten feet to her, and she catches him in her arms.

As they walk, talking about their experiences in the corporal and other realms they've encountered the garden starts to fade, disappearing into the ether. As the lane grows in front of them, new worlds are created under their feet, universes coming to life with words and emotions expressed to the world around them. The gods walk forward, never looking backwards.

PRIMAL

The smell of the woods filled my snout; poking ahead of me in the dark, it drew in the overpowering scent of the falling leaves and the earth under my paws. I ran, smelling small animals, a deer to the far left of me and the occasional owl overhead. The woods had been freshly reinvigorated by the warm spring that we were experiencing this year. It had that earthy, freshly rained smell, and I loved it. I was a city person, but I loved my country house. It was quiet, and I could be myself without the fear of people spying on me.

I wasn't hungry, at least not for food. I'd traversed the woods behind my house for years, hunting and looking for someone to fuck. In these woods, people like me roamed; people just a bit more...primal. I smelled something strange ahead of me, it was a big cat like me, but somehow different, something I'd never smelled before. The spicy pheromones it put off were blanketing the woods. This female big cat was spraying the woods looking for a partner. My nose flared as I breathed it in. I felt myself starting to shift without any thought. I took the form of a Bengal tiger, my chosen form. I dropped to all fours, my arms and hands changing first, the fur and claws popping out. The transitions are painless and faster than the movies show. In seconds my vision shifted and I could see more in the dark. My hind legs reshaped and I was changed. I ran on faster, feeling the still alien muscles flowing like liquid steel under my flesh and fur.

Shifters like me are born this way. We don't choose to be able to change our form at will; it's a glitch in our genetics. Most people don't realize they are able until it happens, but folks like me often had family members that taught us about it, how to control it. We were the lucky ones.

My eyes picked up the smallest amount of light and showed me things that my human form couldn't. The pitch black woods I was running in looked like twilight in my vision, trees and shrubs visible as I sprinted. Suddenly I saw a flash of white ahead of me, darting between trees. I looked closer as I ran; it looked like an albino panther. I pushed myself harder, the dirt and leaves flicking behind me as my claws dug into the earth below me.

I was in a copse of pine trees, and the pine was overpowering my scent. The pheromones of the big cat mingled with the pine and I spun around. I was smelling and looking for the flash of white, but I couldn't see it. I grew angry and I pawed at the earth. The aroma of the soil cleansed my nose as I leaned down and sniffed deeply. I slowly closed and opened my eyes. As I looked ahead I saw something.

There, further on, I had another glimpse of the large white cat. She was stopped and her hindquarters were in the air. I stared, trying to figure out what she was doing. Her forepaws and head were on the ground, but her hind was wiggling. She was next to a tree, marking it, so I slowly paced in a zigzag pattern as I walked close to her. I was being cautious because poachers had been known to employ shifters to entice real animals in the wild. She turned her head and growled at me. I took it as an invite to come closer.

I ran up to her and started circling. She was an albino panther as I thought. I paced closer, breathing deep. I was in the middle of Ohio, outside of a lost cougar and a few bobcats there were no big cats here, at least not counting lycanthropes, and this creature didn't smell like one of those. Her rump almost wagged in anticipation, and I felt my tiger body respond.

I circled her, taking a swipe in her direction to see if she was going to respond negatively to me. The pink eyes followed me and she growled. I walked up to her, sniffed her face and neckline. I didn't smell any other male on her, and I walked to her raised rump. Burying my nose in her groin I smelled deeper, and she shifted her body.

I felt it before I could see it. She was shifting, changing from albino panther to human. I sat on my hindquarters as I watched.

Her white fur seemed to melt from her, sliding upwards, starting with her back legs. The flesh and fur on her feet slid forward, leaving human feet and calves. It was fully fleshed, unlike some lycanthrope changes when they're younger. The calves of her legs appeared, and slowly slid up. The panther flesh was sliding forward, slowly and methodically. Across her ass and groin, now lower back and stomach. The pheromones I smelled earlier were coming from her, the human form. I stood and started pacing behind her, and her panther head shook in a very human gesture. I stopped, fighting the desire to lean forward and lick her wetness with my large tongue. The flesh was sliding forward and as her teats turned into breasts, I growled in need. Next were her shoulders and arms, then her head and hands. As the transformation ended, there was a pile of fur and flesh lying in front of her.

Her human form was beautiful; a full figured woman with long white hair, that was perfectly natural. She looked to be in her early forties, but didn't have a line on her face that she didn't want. In the corners of her eyes were small, but beautiful, crow's feet, laugh lines surrounded her mouth. She laid out with her former form under her, laying on it, propped up by her elbows. She smiled with the confidence of someone who was used to being in charge. Her long hair flowed around her shoulders, framing her body. She reminded me of someone, but I couldn't figure out who.

"Are you human?"

I started to change; my transformation was similar to hers, but quicker. First my muscular legs and calves appeared and then I stood, the flesh sliding upwards and defying gravity. My thighs and hips appeared, and my cock erect. I raised my arms above my head, and roared. We were a good ten to fifteen miles from any humans, so no one would hear. Finally I was me, a heavy stomach the only flaw on my athletic frame. My long black hair laid flat on my back as I threw my transformation flesh to the ground.

I walked forward, and she licked her lips. I stepped forward slowly, trying to make sure she didn't get freaked out by me, but she smiled in the dark, her eyes shining. I could make out her form on the panther fur as the moon broke from behind the clouds. The trees above were illuminated with the moonlight and beams fell around us. Still reclined, her right hand beckoned me. She looked at me, from my feet to my head, and nodded once, as if to say I would do.

"Is that your normal size? I want it to fill me."

I stared at her in disbelief. She had a power about her. It was turning me on, but it pushed me at the same time. Her allure and sexuality was like a cloud of fog around her. She had this darkness to her, a need that I wasn't sure if I could fill. I loved it rough but she might want it rougher than I could give. If she wanted to fuck a big dicked guy, she could have gone to a bar and found one. I made my shock and anger known with a low growl.

"What the fuck?"

"Make your cock thicker! You're a shifter, dammit!" She lifted her right hand, showing me how thick she wanted my cock. I looked into her eyes, and beneath the command I could see an edge of pleading, so I decided to try.

I blinked a few times then focused. I closed my eyes, and forced my penis to grow from the three inch thickness it already was to about five inches thick. I felt my heart increase in size to support the growth, and it hurt like heartburn. I swallowed, and the pain disappeared.

She let out a low, deep chuckle and it turned me on. I walked over to her, heartbeat pounding and my cock slick with pre-come as I worked myself up. The thickness was strange in my hand, but I wanted her too much to debate the issue. I got on my knees, still stroking my cock as she spread her legs. Bracing myself with one hand on the albino fur, I let go and run my left hand up from the bottom of her pussy to her clit. Spreading her outer lips with my pointer and middle finger, I leaned down to her and smelled her heady scent, cedar and something spicy. Lycanthropes smelled different from normal humans, usually more earthy.

I leaned forward, exploring her sex with my tongue. I started licking her clit, just the exposed tip. Her hands went to my hair. She moaned softly as I licked her, exploring both sides of her clit for the best spot. I knew I'd found it when she gasped and started moaning loudly, making my cock harder than it was already. The moans that came from her turned me on. I flicked my tongue at the sweet spot I'd found, and I made her come once, twice. Her legs would have clamped around my head if my shoulders weren't in the way. I was hunched up as I kept going, making her come one more time. I pulled away; her strange eyes glittering in the dark. My eyes were still adapted for the woods, but I didn't think they shone quite like hers.

She lifted her legs away from me and raised them, spread apart. I took her ankles in my hands, and spread them further. She started to roll her hips as I moved closer, and I started to slip inside of her. It was difficult, my thickness filling her tight pussy. I eased my tip into her slick opening and she shook her head, annoyed.

"Fuck me, I don't have long!"

I became irrationally angry, and I slammed the fullness of my cock into her as she asked. She gasped as I filled her. I felt her heat and wetness as I started pounding her, she soly focused on stretching to accommodate me. I fucked her harder with each thrust, and her fingernails dug furrows into my shoulders, down my back, and across my ass. The pain drove me harder, my cock like a diamond. My breath came from me in insane gasps, punctuated with swears and growls.

"Who the fuck are you?"

She let out a string of unintelligible comments, punctuated with a *fuckmeohgod* that ultimately was all I could make out. She started to thrust upward towards me when I slowed for a moment. Her strange eyes shined brighter in the darkness. I hadn't come yet, and I needed to. She hadn't either, and I almost felt like I failed her somehow.

"My ass, please, my ass."

I growled, deep and vibrating. I'm not sure if I wanted to make her come now, or if I just wanted her ass. She made the choice for me, pulling her fingernails from my ass and shoving me off of her. She flipped over and spread her legs, looking back at me. I climbed back onto the fur and gripping my cock with my right hand, I braced her left hip with the other. I shoved it in; still as thick as when her pussy had taken it. She stiffened, and I could feel her screaming in pleasure as I sunk in all the way to my balls. She lifted her head and moaned again, writhing in the pleasure and pain she wanted.

"Do it! Make me feel you! *Fill* me!" She turned around to look at me, urging me on. Thrusting back, she started gasping louder as the orgasm rolled through her. I felt her clench in pleasure as her hands tore at the fur. Each thrust back she loosened more, and I wasn't comfortable with the blood leaking from her orifice. She glanced back, anger showing on her face.

"Fine, I'll do it!"

I was deep in her, and as she started to buck back, my hands went to her shoulders. Taking several deep breaths, I started to thrust as hard and fast as I could. She was tighter again, and if I didn't know any better I'd say she'd made herself tighter. Her face was buried in the fur of her animal form, but I could hear her as she gasped and screamed. Suddenly something changed, and I couldn't keep going, her ass loosened as I thrust. Her head rose, and she glared back at me, growling in pleasure as she gripped the white fur beneath her. My right hand snaked down to her pussy. I played with her clit, wanting to come inside her. She sprayed fluids all over my hand, and started moaning louder as I matched her.

We gasped and thrust in time, and soon I came. The pressure built in the base of my cock, and I spurted several times. She growled in pleasure, a hint of panther in it. Her eyes glowed again when she looked back at me, her long hair bobbing in time with her thrusts backwards. I kept going, able to stay hard as long as I wanted.

I felt a second orgasm building, and I pulled out of her. I grabbed her legs, and flipped her over onto her back. I made my cock grow a little bit more, and then I plunged it into her, her long legs thrown over my shoulders. I bit her calves and squeezed her thighs between thrusts. I dropped her legs and while I pounded, I leaned down and started biting and pinching her nipples with my teeth and fingers, the inner edges of her breasts, the bottoms, and outer edges. My hands ended up on her shoulders again, and I thrust until I came.

She lay there, feeling my orgasm spray into her, and she started weeping gently.

"Thank you. He won't do this for me. Thank you."

Somehow, the knowledge of another man turned me off. I wanted to throw her from me, but I stood up, forcing my cock to shrink to its normal size. I pulled the old flesh off like a used condom and threw it deep into the woods again. Bending over, I stared at her as I gripped the white fur under her. I yanked it as hard as I could, and she flopped off of it onto the ground. I walked back to where I'd originally changed and picked mine up. I offered it to her, and she took it. She walked over to me, legs wobbly and fluids coming from her pussy, running down her leg. I growled deeply, as she snatched it from my hands.

I turned and walked away; angrier than I was when I began

my hunt tonight. I started to run, wrapping the white fur around my chest and waist, a makeshift toga. I had about six miles to go until I reached the edge of my property. Running was easier than normal, my heart still large from the growth. I saw my house, the lonely back porch light on. I ran toward it, the light becoming my sole focus, and as I entered the light on the edge of the woods I was my human form.

It's been several months since I walked or stalked the woods looking for her, knowing that I was able to give her what she needed.

THE SWITCH

Alex woke up feeling strange, as if he weren't in his own body. He opened his eyes and looked down. He was nude, and saw with a second glance that he really *wasn't* himself. He had a pair of decent sized breasts which shivered and broke out in goose bumps as the cold air from the fan rolled over him, the nipples erect. He rolled over, looking down the length of his body. He had a mound of pubic hair and when he felt himself, he discovered that there were other changes as well. He had to pee so he ran to the bathroom, slapping his ass on the toilet. It was an unfamiliar sensation, strange and a bit different. He looked down at his breasts, they were heavier than he expected. He gave one of them a playful bounce or two as he thought, trying to figure out what happened.

He remembered going to bed, dreaming of being a woman, and now he'd woken up as one. He wiped - *front to back* - and flushed. Then he stood up, and looked at himself in the mirror. He was pleased to find that he was good looking. He ran his hands down his body, unsure of what the hell he was going to do but an idea came to him. He spoke a simple sentence, and it was a feminine voice that came out.

It was his day off so the idea forming sounded like a good one; he had time to see what he could do. Unsure of just how he had changed, Alex wasn't convinced he was fully sure of what happened, but as he leaned on the edge of the counter staring at his newly nude body he was becoming more accustomed to the idea of being a woman. It should be simple right?

He decided he would get dressed in whatever would work

for him and go out. It was close to seven pm, as the whole night was before him, Alex had an idea and his night shift employment usually gave him the right free time to do what he wanted. Before he got dressed in his nicest clothes, he sat down on the edge of the bed. Laying back, he started exploring his newly discovered vagina and breasts, trying to learn what felt the best.

***

He drove to a club he had seen, but one he had never really been to before; the prospect always exciting and scaring him when he'd gone past during his normal everyday life. It was a swingers club which he'd heard also had a small BDSM community. He parked a few streets over and grabbed some cash, but then he stopped and thought about the ID issue. He didn't have one for a woman, his was for a man. *Fuck it; I'll suck someone off if I have to. Would he? Yeah, it's why he was here if he wanted to be honest.*

He walked up to the door and stood there a few seconds, unsure of what to do. Then he grabbed the handle and opened the door. It was setup like a diners club or a country club. There was a receptionist and a guard standing nearby. They were talking about normal things. He walked up to the desk and stood there, waiting.

"How many tonight?" The receptionist asked, in a soothing voice.

"Just one." He said, his voice shaking as he quivered in excitement and fear.

"It's fifty five for a one night pass, but if you want we can set you up with other plans."

He pulled the cash out and paid the woman sixty. She quietly made the change and handed it to him. Along with the cash came a rubber arm band like the ones people sell for fund raisers. He looked at it and saw it said Monday Female in the middle of the black and white material. He slipped it on, and the guard opened the right double door with a nod and a polite smile.

It opened into a dining room with a large bar on the right. Quiet music played, soft and low as he walked in. People stopped and looked at him for a moment, and then went back to drinking or eating. There wasn't anything insane going on like he imagined. Nobody was giving blow jobs in the room, or fucking wildly on the furniture. There must be some private rooms, or else this was just some sort of a meet up place. There were people dressed like him, in the nicest clothes or in fancy outfits. Everyone was mingling and talking, and there was a low murmur in the room. He walked over to the bar and when the bartender came over, he ordered a whiskey on the rocks.

He received his drink and leaned against the bar, trying to thrust his breasts out. He didn't have a bra on, and he hoped it got him attention. He looked around and saw that there was a table of guys who kept looking towards him. He considered it a minute and then a hint of movement caught his eye. He looked at the door as a man walked in, nervous and scared, like him. The man walked to the bar a few stools down from him and ordered something light, a wine cooler. Not catching much interest, he turned back towards the five guys staring at him at the table. He walked over, noting that they looked like office workers.

The tall man in the center with the dark blond hair was the most attractive, and looking at him he felt a heat growing between his legs. He stared at him out of that pretty face and the man stared back. He decided to take the empty seat, plopping down with a jiggle that was more than a little intentional.

"You guys want to play a game? It's my first time here, where are all the sex rooms? Where do you go?"

The tall blond stared at her, and cleared his throat.

"All of us? Or just one of us. The rooms are in the back."

"All of you."

Everyone stared at Alex, at the table. Then the tall man stood, and the others did too. Alex was the last to stand, knees shaky. His ass looked good in the jeans he was wearing, and he hoped it was still nice when those pants were off. They fell into a single line, and he was last. She glanced back, and saw the man with the wine cooler was staring at her. He was nice looking, but not as nice as the blonde. The other guys she was following had boring hair, except for the larger bald guy.

The doors leading to the hallway with the rooms was non-descript, a metal door with a large knob. They stepped into the hallway, it was wide and quiet. There were red door knob hangers on the doors that were presumably occupied, and green on the empty. He took the lead, opening the green doors on the left, looking for something specific. There were doors with red tags on the handles, and he guess those were occupied rooms. He tried several doors that were tag free. Four doors down he found it, and he turned to the men with a coy smile.

"Are you okay with bondage? I want to play a game."

They all stood there, nodding in silence. The blond kept his eyes on him, and he felt scared for a moment.

"Safe word?" The blond asked quietly.

"Amulet"

The man with glasses cleared his throat, staring at him.

"What's your name? Mine is Gordon, and he's Adam" motioning with his head he nodded towards the blond man.

The third man has a small clover tattoo on his arm, and he said he was simply Clover. He didn't think much about it, but it was odd that the nickname he gave the guy was his name.

The men all nodded, and he had a feeling they might have done this before. He opened the door and grabbed the red hanger, placing it over the green. They all fell into the room in silence. He walked to the middle of the room and looked around. There was a bed with restraints attached to the side of it, and in the center of the room was a chain dangling from the ceiling with a large bolt holding it up. There was a loop hanging from the chain. There were dressers and a closet too. He walked over to the closet and opened it. There were all kinds of toys on shelves and racks. He found a longer chain and a pair of handcuffs. He took them out and started unbuttoning his shirt. He undid his belt and the button on his pants, turning to look at them.

"Get naked, all of you." He spoke with a confidence he hadn't felt a moment before, a confidence he'd been lacking in so many areas of his life up until this moment.

The men started undressing. He noticed that the named Adam was taking his time, and the slow reveal of his naked body was exciting. Long and lightly muscular, the mans body was covered in light colored body hair. As he watched the Adonis undress, he felt his vagina begin to get wet, the nipples under the shirt beginning to tighten a little from the cool air and arousal both. His woman's body didn't demand the same sort of attention that the man's one had; the desire spreading out from his groin yes, but with so much more going on as well, it radiated out, touching on erogenous zones he hadn't dreamed a woman had before tonight.

He dropped the button up shirt and walked to the chain, looping the four foot chain through the loop, and then attached the clip to the center link on the handcuffs. Alex put one hand in, and closed it around his wrist. It's tight, but not uncomfortable. Then he motioned to Gordon to do the other one. Soon he was on his knees, breasts heaving as he took deep breaths. He was so scared, but excited to be experiencing this strange anomaly. His heart pounded away under his skin, nipples harder even more in the chilly air, his skin one big live wire of tingling anticipation. He closed his eyes for a breath and looks at them to speak.

"I want you to start beating off on my chest, my tits. Last one to come gets to fuck my pussy. Then we'll decide what we do."

The men circled in front of him, and Alex watched the different shaped and sized cocks bobbing and being manipulated.

Gordon comes first, and he backs away, ashamed. Clover is next, large spurts coating his hand and shaft. He slips away, rubbing his come covered hand on his thigh. Adam came last, spraying come onto his left nipple, thick and hot. Alex looks up at Adam his pleasure evident on his face, and Adam walks to the closet.

He grabs something small and comes back, it's the key. Alex shakes his head, and stares at Adams half hard cock. Adam moves closer, Alex eagerly takes him into his mouth. Alex wraps the lips of his alien body around it and starts bobbing, keeping his teeth away from the hot flesh. Before he knows it, he's swallowing come, not really tasting it. He pulled away, staring up. Adam smiles deeply, and runs his hand along his left cheek, down to the rounded chin. He shivers at this touch from the Adonis. Clover takes the key and releases the limbs locked into place.

His arms and hands are feeling strained and gravity pulls his left hand down, thumping off his breast as it's released. He starts massaging the semen from the men into where it landed the fluids sticky and cold in his fingertips now. He stands and walks over to the bed, ass swinging in the air. He climbs onto the bed, spreading swollen labia open for Adam.

He feels Adam slip inside; filling him and, the comparison between being entered versus entering another is strange at first. Tingling warmth begins to spread inside him, slipping up from his new core up over the clit which gives its own more subtle response and then it shivers out into the rest of his flesh, beginning to build. He starts moaning as the large cock is pounding into him, loud and sharp gasps coming out of his mouth as it taps his G-spot. His anus is being played with, first one finger, and then as it opens, two. He's thrusting back against the blonde's thrusts, and the sensation of his vagina and anus being manipulated is too much, sending electricity through his nervous system and making him twitch as he squirts vaginal fluid across the bed under him. Burying his face in a pillow, he screams and keeps thrusting back. Blond is wrapping his hands around his breasts and pinching the nipples. He freezes, the sensations too much as he comes again.

Adam comes once, twice, three times. Stiffening, he pulls out and sits on the bed. Alex collapses on his stomach, ass in the air. Gasping deep and hard, he turns and looks at the room. The other men are staring, and in a moment Clover comes over, rubbing his cock hard. Laying there in the afterglow, he begins to feel a small shiver of something build back up within him. Clover and a now hard Gordon are running their hands over him, pulling and pushing the right spots. The warm lube is spread across his anus, inside and fingers open him. The two fingers in his ass feel good, filling. Wanting more, he spreads his legs and Clover climbs on the bed and straddles him. He gasps as the thicker cock slowly pushes in, pausing a moment to let his body adjust.

Motioning to Gordon, he beckons him over and Alex takes him into mouth. While sucking off Gordon, Clover applies more lube from the stand next to the bed, pulling himself out, coating his condom covered cock more. Clover slides in easier now and starts thrusting hard and fast, reaching around and fingering his clit. Moaning while Clover fucks his ass, he starts bobbing faster and sucking harder on Gordon, who comes hard and fast. He tastes the fluid, and this time it's bitter, but he swallows and pulls the cock from his mouth. Running the tip of the cock around his lips he dives back in. The hands on his hips are gripping tighter, the thrusts pushing him into the bed. He's enjoying the sensations, and he comes twice, feeling more hands on his body. He slips Clover out of him and feeling spontaneous, he kisses Gordon hard on the lips.

The men pull from away from him, clearly spent for some time. She motions over to Adam, whose been watching from the side of the bed.

"I want to watch you men fuck each other."

They all stand there, looking at each other for a moment, then Adam takes the lead. Taking Gordon's hand and placing it on his hard on, he kisses him hard and deep. Hands start exploring each other, a wild abandonment happening in the seconds it takes the three to realize he was enjoying the show. The alien voice cracks as it speaks.

"Suck him off Adam!"

Adam drops to his knees, taking Gordon and Clover's hard members into his hands. He starts stroking them, kissing the tip every other stroke of each men. Adam stops after a few minutes, focusing on stroking both men to orgasm.

Suddenly everything slows down, the two men coming at once, but the world shifts. As Adonis scrunches his face up in anticipation, everything freezes.

Standing beside the bed, he turns, looking around. The room is frozen, and the world is collapsing upon its self. As the world is shrinking into a pinpoint of bright, white light, the man stands there, feeling a pulling sensation. A sudden snap in the universe and he's lying in bed.

The white, cracked ceiling is above him like it had been earlier and he feels normal. Lifting the sheets, he feels the normal sensation of morning wood. Reaching down and grasping his cock, he starts stroking himself, his other hand reaching to his balls. Gasping as he comes quickly, thinking of the sensations from less than a few minutes ago, it squirts into the sheets. Not caring he keeps stroking, and comes again quickly. Orgasm over, he throws the sheet off of him and stands. Walking to the bathroom naked, he looks at himself in the mirror. Alex is himself again. What occurred? Had it been real? Was it just an extremely lucid dream?

The phone ringing brings him out of those thoughts. Running towards his cell he forgets the sensations and answers, slipping back into his old life without a thought.